Also by Julie B. Cosgrove

Wordplay Mysteries

Word Has It
Word Gets Around
In Other Words
Hang on Every Word
Away With Words
Loss for Words

Relatively Seeking Mysteries

One Leaf Too Many
Fallen Leaf
Leaf Me Alone

Bunco Biddies Mysteries

Dumpster Dicing
Baby Bunco
Threes, Sixes & Thieves
'Til Dice Do Us Part

The Visitor Mysteries

The Visitor Makes a Retreat

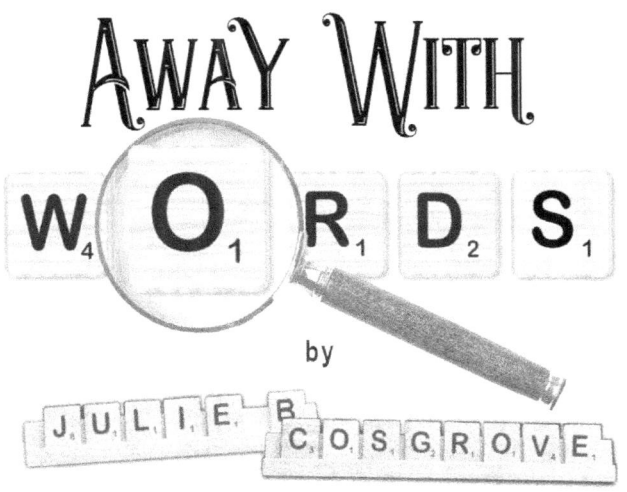

AWAY WITH

W O R D S

by

JULIE B COSGROVE

P

Write Integrity Press, LLC

Away With Words
© 2023 Julie B Cosgrove

ISBN: 978-1-951602-21-5

 Published by Pursued Books:
an imprint of Write Integrity Press, LLC
PO Box 702852
Dallas, TX 75370

Find out more about the author, Julie B Cosgrove, at her website: www.juliebcosgrove.com
or on her author page at www.WriteIntegrity.com.

Printed in the United States of America.

Dedication

Dedicated to my friend and extraordinary Medieval epic author Katy Huth Jones for the grace she displays to me and others in her life. Thank you for your support and camaraderie, and for often playing Scrabble with me over hot tea, chicken salad, and English biscuits as we discuss plot twists and life in general.

Contents

CAST OF CHARACTERS

Wanda Lee Warner – A widow who loves word games. She has lived in Scrub Oak, TX, most of her life. She has a keen wit and a natural curiosity about events in her town because she loves her community and its residents. She has a dachshund named Sophie.

Betty Sue Simpson – Wanda's best friend since they were kids. She is also a widow. As a retired elementary school teacher, she knows the background of almost everyone who has lived in town since 1965. She also likes word games and puzzles.

Evelyn Joseph – Wanda's next-door neighbor who moved to Scrub Oak ten years ago to care for her sister until she passed away from cancer. The widow of an Army Intelligence officer, who was killed in the Gulf War in 1990, she never remarried. She stayed in Scrub Oak because she and Wanda became good friends and she wanted to finally put down roots.

Todd Martin – Wanda's nephew, who returned to Scrub Oak to join the police force. They have always been close and enjoy a good game of Scrabble together on Thursday mornings before his shift. He lived with Wanda during his high school years while his parents divorced.

Fred Ballinger – The retired principal of Scrub Oak's high school. He has eyes for Betty Sue.

Vicki Clyburn – The daughter of the previous *Oakmont County Weekly Gazette* owner, Tom Jacobs. Married to Mason, mother to baby Ian.

Mason Clyburn – Vicki's husband who has a business degree and a second degree in journalism. He has taken over as the Chief Editor at *The Gazette* and digitalized it, with Tom's blessings.

Jake Overby – Summer intern at *The Gazette.*

Olga Westheimer – One of the ladies on the retreat who loves to solve mysteries, too. Her late husband was a renowned mystery author.

George McDavid, and his wife **Rachel** – own the retreat center and land surrounding it. He is a retired forensic scientist. Their grandson, Flex, was on the West Monroe High wrestling team until he graduated a few weeks back.

Mary Jane Smithers – Retreat leader.

Martha Raymond – Retreat coordinator.

And lead us not into temptation
but deliver us from evil.
Matthew 6:13(ESV)

CHAPTER 1

Wanda Lee Warner let out a shaky sigh as she scanned what had once been her kitchen. The charred stove had been removed, along with the counters, the cabinets, and the other appliances. The bare wall studs gaped like a sinister smile with missing teeth. All her memories from the past thirty some-odd years had been stripped away.

"Look on the bright side." Her best friend, Betty Sue's voice played in her mind as they had glared a few days ago at the smoky mess taped off as a crime scene. "You have been wanting to redo this kitchen for ages."

Right. So, I'd better get with it. She shuffled through the jagged and charred opening that led into the formal dining room and slunk into a Chippendale-styled chair. As she flipped through the pictures of quartz countertops in the flier from the mega home improvement store out on the highway, she felt a stress headache squeezing her temple.

"What was so wrong with harvest gold anyway?"

She had thought it okay when she and her late husband first entered the room while house hunting in 1984. Much cheerier than the copper toned ones everyone wanted back then. Wanda had gasped with delight at the eat-in kitchen with the corner window over the sink. The sunlight filtered through onto the shiny white tiles that covered the counters then extended up in rows as a backsplash. Every fifth tile on the fourth row held a painted pineapple, the symbol of hospitality. The golden speckled linoleum floor, a few shades lighter than the wheat-colored refrigerator, stove, and dishwasher, had made her clap her hands in delight.

"Can we afford this?" Her question had barely moved past her lips as her husband, Big Bill, hugged her four-month-pregnant body and assured her they could now that he had received a promotion. Their three-year old son had spun around the room and landed on his bottom in laughter in the exact spot where her dinette set would perfectly fit. Sold.

And now, almost forty years later, it had all been stripped away thanks to a bomb placed in her oven. Payment for trying to discover the latest crime culprit in her community of Scrub Oak, Texas.

She plopped her chin in her hand. "Oh, well, Big Bill. It's only a kitchen. I have my memories no matter what." Even though widowed eleven years now, she still occasionally chatted with her late hubby. After all those decades together, it seemed to be more of a habit than a gesture of mourning. The ache of his absence had long since sweetened into a ritual.

Wanda set the samples down. Maybe she could duplicate the kitchen all over again. Did they make appliances in harvest gold anymore?

Nope, wouldn't be the same.

A tippity tap sounded on her backdoor. Evelyn, her next-door neighbor, and temporary landlord while the reconstruction commenced, stood on her stoop. Friends in Scrub Oak never came to the front door unless they brought bad news or condolences.

Wanda walked into the shell of her kitchen and motioned her neighbor inside.

Ev wiped her feet, out of habit Wanda assumed. Not much damage one could do to the subflooring at this point.

"Made a decision?"

"Kinda. I've ordered white cabinets. I'm thinking of quartz counters and this Moroccan tile backsplash." She held up the design piece in hues of ecru, navy, and muted green. "I know a lot of people are decorating with gray and black, but I think it's depressing. I want something soothing. And I am thinking of adding those open shelves around the corner windows, and maybe opening up this wall into the dining room since it's half blown up anyway." She motioned with her hands. "And putting in a kitchen island with the sink in it instead of it being crouched in the corner.

Seems to be the in thing now."

"Uh, huh."

Wanda chuckled. Fashion and style never hit her neighbor's radar. She'd probably asked out of courtesy instead of curiosity. "You agree only because you want me to make a final decision, so I can get on with this and eventually move out of your guestroom."

"I'm hurt you'd think so." Evelyn stabbed her fist into her heart and winked.

"I think it would look great! You'll love a huge island with bar stools. Definitely go with that tile to match the soft seafoam green wall paint you showed me." Betty Sue's sing-song voice rang out from the still-open backdoor. She waved her fingers when Evelyn and Wanda turned in her direction. "And I'd pick floor tiles that look like white-washed wood."

Wanda's shoulders relaxed. "Okay. Done."

Betty Sue's blue eyes twinkled as she entered the demolished-back-to-the-studs room and nodded as if visualizing it as she'd just described. Then she tiptoed away from ground zero into the dining room to join them. "Good news. I checked with Martha Raymond, and they have room for three more at the women's retreat in West Monroe this week. Starts Thursday afternoon and ends Sunday morning. She sent me pictures of the cabin. It has five bedrooms and three baths upstairs and two bedrooms and a bath on the main floor. Comfortably sleeps fifteen or more. It is deep in the woods of northern Louisiana near a gurgling brook and overlooks a small pond."

She flipped through her phone to the photos she wanted and held one up. "It's a shame your friend, DiAne can't come."

"Yeah. She's dog-sitting for a neighbor who had emergency surgery." Wanda squinted at the tiny screen. She had to admit the scene oozed with peacefulness. Tall evergreen trees, verdant rolling lawns, and a shimmering body of water with a wooden raft in the center for sunbathing. Adirondack chairs speckled the grounds in front of a screened-in porch running the back length of the modern log cabin.

"It's only two-hundred dollars per person for four days and three nights. That includes meals, though we are asked to help cook, clean up, and bring snacks."

"I don't know . . ."

Betty Sue tucked her lower lip in her teeth, her eyes pleading. "Wanda, it's only four days. A five-hour drive away. If we left at ten on Thursday morning and stopped for lunch in Longview, we'd be there in time for registration at four."

Wanda glanced at her friends. If she ordered what she had decided on today it would take a week to deliver it all. She'd be back well before the contractor began the renovations. "Okay, but only if you come with me to pick out appliances, Betty Sue. I could use your opinion."

Betty Sue squealed with delight. Then she swiveled toward Evelyn. "You're coming, too, right?"

"Appliance shopping? No way. On the retreat? I don't know. Maybe." Evelyn's brows scrunched.

Betty Sue placed a hand on her shoulder. "Come on, Ev. It'll be fun. We haven't been on a road trip in ages. Gloria promised she would check in on Tweety every morning before she heads to open the Bird Nest and every evening after she closes. And if he gets lonely, she will take his cage to the store so the customers can talk to him. He will be in good hands."

Wanda nodded. "And I'm sure Todd will keep an eye out on both of our properties when he comes by to feed Sophie before and after his patrol." Her nephew had been a policeman with the Scrub Oak PD for almost two years now.

"But who will take our places on the neighborhood watch? What if another crime—"

"True." Wanda took her position as chairperson of the town's neighborhood watch program seriously and had recruited Evelyn as one of the captains. Maybe they shouldn't leave town so soon after the last crime wave.

"Collin is back from his and Claudia's anniversary cruise. He would be happy to fill in now that he's retired." Betty Sue continued to knock down their objections.

Evelyn and Wanda eyed each other.

Evelyn puffed a breath from her cheeks. "She's got us,

you know."

Betty Sue's mouth spread into a Cheshire Cat grin. "And, guess what?" She wiggled her eyebrows. "They are having a scavenger hunt. Each team has to solve the crossword puzzle clues, then find the items somewhere on the property."

That cinched it. Wanda Lee Warner never could turn down an opportunity to solve word puzzles. Betty Sue knew that fact all too well. Wanda raised her hands in surrender. "Okay. I'll call Fix It Finn and let him know what I've picked out for the countertop, flooring, and backsplash. You call Martha and confirm our reservations. Then we'll head to the appliance depot."

"Perfect." Betty Sue jiggled her keys. "I'll drive."

"On the way, can we stop off at *The Gazette* and turn in my word puzzles for the week?" Wanda had recently been hired to design both Find a Word in Words and Hangman puzzles for the local county paper. Even though some of the clues had jived with a few robberies, the townsfolk still loved them. Or so Wanda hoped.

As she slid into Betty Sue's car and waved goodbye to Evelyn, excitement began to effervesce in Wanda's veins. With her generous insurance settlement, she could afford a side-by-side fridge with a water and ice dispenser in the door. Maybe a new five-burner gas stove and one of those new drawer-styled microwave ovens, if she found some on sale that is.

She stuck her hand out the window, feeling the not quite ninety-degree summer breeze swish through her fingers. "Thanks for pushing me into going on this retreat, Betty Sue. It'll feel good to get away, and besides, Todd has developed excellent detective skills. If anything pops up, he can probably handle it. If not, I'll only be a phone call away."

"Of course."

Did she hear Betty Sue chuckle under her breath as they turned down Cedar toward 7th Street?

CHAPTER 2

Thursday morning arrived. Since Betty Sue knew where they were headed in northern Louisiana and suffered from mild carsickness, Wanda suggested she sit up front with her while Evelyn sprawled her long legs across the back seat.

They stopped off at a mega gas station with three restaurants under roof on I-20 near Longview a little before noon. After a barbeque lunch, the three wandered the aisles of the convenience store grabbing fudge, chips and dips, and two 12-packs of soft drinks as their contribution for the four-day adventure. Evelyn purchased a clip-on sun visor and SPF30 lotion. Betty Sue spotted a tie-died sunburst T-shirt and rushed to the cashier with a grin. Wanda gave into temptation and bought a pair of white-rimmed sunglasses to accent her evolving salt and pepper hair. Solving three major crimes, being kidnapped, and having her house bombed over the past two years had taken its toll but she still refused to dye it.

With full tummies and shopping sacks draping their arms, the three headed for their destination just outside of West Monroe.

At 4:05 in the afternoon, they pulled into the gravel drive, which wound around the pond toward the cabin. More serene in real life than in the photos, Wanda took in a deep breath and felt the past two weeks of stress slide off her shoulders like pats of butter plopped onto a stack of freshly griddled pancakes.

"Welcome to Embracing Grace's women's retreat." A petite lady with gray, curly hair greeted them with such a huge wave it raised her thin frame to her tiptoes. "You must be Betty Sue, Evelyn, and Wanda from Texas."

"What gave us away? The license plate?" Evelyn scoffed under her breath.

Wanda shushed her as she turned off the ignition.

The lady extended her right hand. "I'm Martha. Please go on inside and meet everyone. You can get your room assignment and freshen up. We start in an hour."

In the entry to the expansive living room with two L-shaped couches facing a stone fireplace, a lady named Janet monitored the check-in table. She handed each of them a packet which contained the names and emails of the other attendees, an agenda, and a one-page bio on the retreat leader Mary Jane Smithers, the author of six video Bible studies, who'd driven up from Baton Rouge. "Here are your name lanyards. You three will share room number five up on the second floor at the far end."

She pointed to a staircase where four women in denim shorts and matching church T-shirts bounced down in sync with their giggles. They looked to be in their early thirties. Wanda wondered if the three of them in their sixties would feel out of place, then she noticed two silver-haired women on the landing that overlooked the living room below.

At five o'clock on the dot, a bell clanged, and the women began gathering like cows called home to the hay barn. Martha drew the drapes to block out the late afternoon sun then clapped her hands to hush the conversations.

"Again, welcome to our weekend entitled Embracing Grace. It is good to see some returning faces as well as new ones. Over the next four days we will learn not only how to accept God's grace more fully but how to better extend it to others. In this day and age of road rage, high anxiety, and me-first attitudes, it is a lesson we all need to relearn, right?"

As Martha peered over her readers at the attendees gathered around her, Wanda envisioned her fourth-grade teacher with a ruler whacking her knuckles if she didn't pay attention.

"You will see a number on the upper righthand corner of your name lanyards." She held hers up and swiveled her hips so the entire room could observe it. Definitely a retired teacher.

"If it is a one, you are in charge of breakfast prep and clean-up every morning. So, arrive in the kitchen at six-thirty tomorrow morning sharp. A two means you are in charge of lunch and should report at eleven-thirty, and the threes have supper duty thus you should be in the kitchen no later than five-thirty in the afternoon tomorrow. Tonight, we have pizza being delivered."

Several, including Wanda, glanced at their name tags. She felt a grin crawl across her lips when she noticed the number three on hers. The weekend may be off to a good start after all.

They proceeded with icebreakers until the pizza delivery guy arrived at six-thirty, poor thing. He appeared to be a high school student and definitely retreated from the room of cackling women as fast as he could politely do so. Even so, Wanda thought his face held a guilt-ridden edge to it. What would he be guilty of at that age? Breaking a Friday night date to make more money, Wanda hoped. Still, she filed her observation in the back of her mind, just in case…

After dinner they went over the rules, the program, and other odds and ends, then watched a short video on grace by a renowned preacher before having a short prayer service and calling it a night.

As Wanda and her friends plodded upstairs, she grabbed a pink lady apple from the snack basket. The jury was still out on how good this retreat would be. Hopefully tomorrow they'd get their crossword puzzle! Then maybe things would pick up.

W

Friday morning after breakfast, Mary Jane led them in a short devotional, reviewed what they had discussed the previous evening, and then handed them the crossword puzzle and clues. "Each clue is a Bible verse but also points to something you can find around here, though you may have to stretch your minds to figure that out. You have an hour and a half to work through it and find as many things as you can. Got it?"

Everyone motioned that they understood.

"Good. Divide up according to your room number. That way there will be five teams of three ladies each. We discourage electronic devices on retreat, but today is an exception. Each team can use one phone . . ." She held up her pointer finger for emphasis. ". . . to take a picture of the item you think matches the clue. We will meet back here when the bell rings at eleven."

Wanda, Evelyn, and Betty Sue grinned at each other as they received their paper. With Wanda's word puzzle skills, Betty Sue's natural eye for wonder, and Evelyn's sharp wit, they had this one in the bag.

"Put your thinking caps on, ladies. The team that returns with the most solved clues receives the 'undeserved favor' of one free pass from their KP duties at any time over the next four days." Mary Jane flashed them a huge smile with her hands clasped in front of her slightly thick waist.

Whistles and applause resounded, but Wanda didn't join in. She had already studied crossword puzzle clues. The first proved easy. Romans 5:20. She knew that without looking it up. It had to do with those who trespass from grace. She filled in T-R-E-S-P-A-S-S. It fit in 1-down. She had seen a no trespassing sign on the entry gate. Easy peasy.

Clue two came from the Psalms. She thumbed through the Bible and read about a deer, a doe. Two squares coming off the e in "trespass" confirmed her answer. Were they to find deer poop? Surely not.

Betty Sue leaned over and whispered. "Where are we to spot a doe?"

Evelyn leaned in. "Maybe in the kitchen? You know, d-o-u-g-h."

"Nah. Spelled differently. I bet there is a painting or a statue of one somewhere in the cabin."

"Good thinking, Betty Sue." Evelyn gave her a wink. "Let's save that one for last since it is probably around here."

Third, started with the "a" off of trespass. She looked up the Proverbs passage. "Apple of your eye"...hmmm. That reminded her to get the apple core out of the trash can before it got pungent.

The fourth one seemed vaguer. Wanda read it out loud as Evelyn and Betty Sue looked on. ". . . grace is poured upon your lips; therefore God has blessed you forever (Psalm 45:2). Hmm."

"Maybe somebody's lip balm?" Betty Sue shrugged.

"I doubt they wants us to rummage through each other's stuff." Wanda tapped the eraser end of the pencil to her temple. "Wait. Grace is *poured.*" She counted the squares down from the "p" in trespass and saw the word fit. "Yep, the answer is poured. Now what pours?"

"How about a pitcher in the kitchen." Betty Sue shrugged.

"Nah. I had breakfast duty. We used all of the pitchers for water, milk, and juice. They're being sterilized in the dishwasher now." Evelyn rested her chin on her hand.

Betty Sue snapped her fingers. "Wait. Down by the brook there is a small waterfall. I heard it when I took my walk this morning. Perhaps pouring refers to water over the rocks?"

"Great thinking." Wanda gave her a high five. "Let's go check it out. If you see a deer on the way, especially a doe, stop and shoot it."

Betty Sue's mouth yanked open. "What?"

"With the camera on Wanda's phone, hon." Evelyn patted her on the shoulder. "No Bambis are in danger today."

Wanda swallowed her desire to chuckle.

The three friends scurried down the path and then through a small clearing where Betty Sue stated she had strayed off the trail because she noticed some pretty pink flowers. Below them, down a fairly steep bank, lay the brook. Just beyond them, the tranquil current began to pick up speed and swirl over some protruding rocks. They followed the bank as the trickling sound increased in volume.

"The waterfall. I knew it." Betty Sue grinned. She snapped a photo.

"Wait. Is that a shoe over there?" Evelyn pointed to a black sneaker with its toe wedged between two rocks in the shallow water.

Wanda edged down the slope sideways to better ensure her balance. She stepped onto one of the rocks and crouched for a better view. "A tennis shoe all right."

"Can you grab it?"

"Think so." She wobbled over the water-splattered rocks to get closer then reached to grab it by the heel and yank it free . . . but, her fingers froze. A red splotch? A chill danced up her arm.

She used her pencil to pry aside the leather tongue under the intertwined laces. The object that caught her attention became more visible in the sunlight filtering through the cypress trees.

Yep, inside the shoe lay a crimson-stained sock. Could it be blood?

GRAPEFRUIT PIE

Ingredients:

- 1¼ cup of sugar
- 1 ¾ cup of water, room temperature
- 2 Tablespoons of cornstarch
- 1/8 teaspoon sea salt
- 1 three-ounce box of strawberry gelatin
- 6 Rio Grande ruby red grapefruit, peeled and sectioned with the seeds and whiteish membranes removed
- 1 nine-inch-deep pie crust, baked – Be sure to prick a few holes in the bottom of the crust with the prongs of a fork so it cooks flat.

Note: Betty Sue made this with a graham cracker crust and it definitely is a good option as long as the crust is thick enough on the bottom.

- Whipped cream for garnish

Directions:

1. Using a large pot over medium heat, cook the sugar, water, cornstarch, and salt, stirring frequently, until thick and clear. Do not boil.
2. Add the box of gelatin and stir until it is thoroughly dissolved. Remove from the heat and set aside until

the gelatin cools and begins to set, about 20-30 minutes.

3. Fold in the grapefruit sections and spoon into the pie crust.

4. Refrigerate for at least one hour before serving. Can be made the day before.

5. Serve with whipped cream if desired. Serves 8.

CHAPTER 3

"Stay there." She cautioned her friends then told them what she'd discovered.

Betty Sue and Evelyn stopped halfway down the bank above her.

Wanda bent to take a picture of the sock and shoe. She knew she shouldn't remove the shoe in case it might be construed as tampering with the evidence.

Evelyn spoke up first, a tad loudly to be heard over the rushing water. "You think it's a crime scene, huh?"

"Oh, Evelyn. You and your thirst for mystery. Maybe someone simply got their foot wedged in the rocks and cut their heel."

Betty Sue, always the optimist. Wanda rose up again. She twisted her torso to scan the area. No left tennis shoe anywhere within her sight. "Perhaps, Betty Sue. It does seem odd that its match isn't somewhere close by."

"Can you tell if it is a man's or a woman's?" Betty Sue cupped her hands around her mouth to make sure her voice carried down the steep incline.

Wanda shrugged. "Kinda non-descript. From the sole it appears to be a hiking shoe." She bent down again and pushed the bloody sock away to see if she could read the size stamped on the side. "Says it is a 9N." She glanced back up the embankment at her friends.

Evelyn dug her phone from her hip pocket. She searched for a signal and found one. A quick internet search revealed the average shoe size for women was an eight, for men a ten and a half. Fewer men wore narrow ones, though. She relayed her findings. "Could be either one, it seems. Large woman or small man. But the narrow size makes me think it's a girl's because it says one-third of women wear narrow shoes."

"Great." Wanda stretched her lower back into an inverted arch and heard a small pop. "Guess we need to report this, then. Can't tell how long it's been in the stream, but my guess is not long since only the toe of the shoe seems wet."

Evelyn called back down to her. "We will go get help. You stay there and guard the shoe in case any of the other teams guess the same clue."

Wanda gave her the "okay" hand signal. She watched as her friends waddled up the bank and disappeared. Then she snatched a stick floating in the stream and poked at the sock. She pulled it up by the elastic edging and stared at it.

Ah, well that explained a lot. And also opened up more questions, too.

She maneuvered the sock back into the shoe then stepped rock by rock across the brook to the bank to perch on a fairly dry cypress root. Questions swirled in her brain, mimicking the water flowing around the toe of the black sneaker.

How long had it been wedged in there?

How often did people hike around here?

Did the brook designate the private property boundary? If so, who owned the land on the other side? She noticed a barb-wired fence running along the top.

How often is the cabin used for retreats and when did the last group stay?

She glanced up at the summer sunrays peeking through the cypress limbs above her head. A cooling breeze rose from the brook and teased the needles on the widespread branches. A whiff of the piney sap filled her nostrils. At any other time, she'd let the peacefulness seep into her soul.

Not today. Wanda groaned and closed her eyelids. *Why does crime always seem to find me?*

A few minutes later she heard voices growing closer. She rose, ready to ward off the next group of clue seekers, then recognized Evelyn's lower pitched tone.

"It's down here. Our friend, Wanda is guarding it."

Leaves and twigs crunched under foot. Wanda brushed

off her tan capris and shaded her eyes with her hand.

Evelyn pointed at her, but had her head turned the way she'd come. Two other women hurried to the bank, led by Betty Sue. She recognized Martha, the one who had greeted them yesterday when they arrived. The second one, a deep redhead with freckles, brought up the rear.

"It's over there." Wanda pointed to the middle of the stream. "We noticed it when the sun hit it."

Martha hesitated as if deciding whether getting her shoes wet would be worth the trek for a closer view. The other lady, tall and slender, tiptoed toward the brook as if the creature from the Black Lagoon would pop out of the water at any minute and grab her.

Wanda checked her own attitude. Perhaps observing possible crime scenes were becoming mundane to her, but that didn't mean they would be to these two ladies. Show grace. The theme of the weekend. She cleared her throat and spoke in the calmest tone she could muster.

"Do either of you recognize the shoe?"

Both shook their heads.

Wanda probed further. "There is no telling how long it has been stuck there. We've not had any rain in weeks in North Texas. How about here?"

"Been dry as dog kibble." The redhead crossed her arms. "By the way, I'm Rachel."

She pronounced it *raw-shell*. The woman explained her presence. She and her husband, George McDavid, were the caretakers of the property. They inherited it from his parents and had turned it into a retreat center. They lived about a half mile up the road and she had arrived with a fresh fruit salad to go with their lunch when Betty Sue and Evelyn entered out of breath looking for Martha.

Wanda extended her hand in a shake and introduced herself. "We were down here because of clue three—grace pours? Betty Sue thought perhaps it meant the waterfall."

"Oh, clever." Martha smiled. "Actually, the clue is drip. The old water pump in the back by the screened in porch drips constantly." Her hand suddenly flew to her mouth as if she'd muttered a curse. "Oops. I shouldn't have told you that."

Wanda waved the awkward moment away. "It's okay. Guess we three have sort of dropped out of the hunt by now anyway." Though she wondered why that would be the answer when the Bible verse clue didn't have "drip" in it. She shoved that query aside for the moment.

"Should we call the police?" Martha glanced at Wanda then Rachel.

"When did the last group stay here?" Wanda shifted her gaze to the caretaker's face.

"Sev . . . several weeks, actually." Rachel stuttered. "Um, ya'll are the first group up here since the third weekend in May. That time . . ." She stopped and swallowed. "Well, they were all friends of our grandson graduating from high school, you see, so we let them have a lock-in of sorts the weekend after senior finals."

Wanda scrunched her mouth to one side. Had the pizza guy been one of them? Did he know something? Surely someone would have noticed the guilt in his eyes the past three weeks. Unless returning here brought it on. She shook the thought away.

"I think we can rule them out, unless someone snuck their girlfriend in." She waded back into the shallow swirl and pulled the sock out of the shoe with the waterlogged stick.

The white knit footwear with crimson-brown stains soaked into it also sported a row of pink apples stitched at the cuff. Definitely not a teenage guy's choice in fashion.

Wanda felt the blood leave her cheeks. The third clue in the crosswords had been an apple…surely not!

All the blood rushed from Rachel's face, too, as she pulled her cell phone from her jeans pocket. "I better call George."

CHAPTER 4

Wanda didn't know what she expected George to look like, but she didn't imagine him to be the man who sauntered over to them and expertly slid down the bank sideways in his waders. A whisp of a man about five foot-four, his wife towered over him by a good three inches. His bald head and light pinkish skin hardly screamed the outdoorsy type. More like an accountant tucked away for decades in the basement of an office building surrounded by racks of boxes and ledgers, Bob Cratchit style.

"Ladies." He nodded, then proceeded to hop over the rocks to the shoe. After a moment he rose and scratched his head. "Definitely not one of yours, my dear, is it?"

His wife opened her mouth, but no words emerged.

Wanda cleared her throat to get his attention. "Let's not jump the gun, here. We haven't asked any of the women on this retreat if it belongs to them. And we can't assume the bloody sock is indicative of foul play, right?"

George glanced up at her as if noticing her for the first time. "You are absolutely correct, Miz—?

"Warner. Wanda Warner."

To her surprise he reached into his khaki shorts pocket and pulled out a pair of blue plastic gloves, the kind surgeons and CSI investigators wore. Then he took several pictures of the shoe at different angles before wiggling it loose from the riverbed.

Evelyn softly whistled. "He knows what he's doing all right."

Rachel edged closer to the trio of guests. "George is a retired forensics specialist."

Betty Sue let out a squeak. "That explains a lot."

The man's esteem leaped four notches in Wanda's opinion. She eased down the bank toward him and across the rocks. By the time she got there, he had tweezered the sock to examine the stain pattern.

"Seems to be stained mostly at the heel wouldn't you say?"

"Hmm." He straightened up and dangled it in front of her. "I would think the wound would be in the area of the ankle and bled down into the shoe."

"Brushed against bramble then?"

His brow crinkled. "I don't think so, my dear lady. Maybe barbed wire or a sharp rock."

Did he suddenly sound like Sherlock Holmes with a

slight Southern drawl to anyone else but Wanda? "Oh?"

"A puncture or cut I surmise. A scrape wouldn't bleed so profusely, would it?" He tilted his head as he scrutinized the cuff. "And brambles would most likely scrape the malleolus, otherwise known as the ankle bone. Plus, there would be organic residue from the plant embedded in the sock fibers. No, I'd think the wound would be higher up, made by something tight and strong enough to cause a gash in the skin."

A chill zipped through Wanda despite the summer sun almost directly above them by now. "You mean like a shackle."

He placed the sock carefully back inside the shoe, then gazed at her with one eyebrow arched. "Presumably so. Though someone could have simply injured the leg while hiking."

Her heart thumped louder in her chest. "But it could be from a restraint. Like the ones used by traffickers?"

His eyebrow returned to its normal position. "Let's not go there yet, all right? However, I am afraid the wearer could have been escaping some kind of danger. Otherwise, why not stop and retrieve her sock and shoe?"

"So, you think foul play might be involved?"

"Seems possible, doesn't it?" George motioned for them to head back up the bank then held out his hand to help Wanda across the stream.

When they reached the other women, George plastered

on a professional smile. "You ladies go on with your retreat. It might be a good idea to make sure no one has lost a shoe or has a nasty cut on their ankles, huh?"

Martha nodded.

He eyed her specifically. "Martha, you are the organizer for the week, yes? Do ask the women not to venture down here for now, okay?"

"Right." Her lips pursed together as if to squelch a question she'd decided not to ask.

He gave her a head bob and then focused on Wanda, Betty Sue, and Evelyn. "And ladies, if I could be bold enough to ask to take a few photos of your shoe treads, that might prove helpful since you have already traipsed around this area."

Each bent their left knee backward as he crouched and took pictures with his phone. Then he thanked them and strolled away. Martha and Rachel followed.

"Is he going to call the police?" Betty Sue fidgeted with her necklace chain.

Wanda laced her arms over her waist. "That would be my guess. I think he suspects something." She sucked in a deep breath and began to observe the ground. She had seen the tread of the black shoe had contained mud and small sprigs of grass. But around here lay mostly cypress leaves and soil. The field stretched above the bank, though. She glanced over the property. Barbed wire rows strung between steel poles encased the boundaries of the retreat area. If she wandered along the perimeter, would she discover slivers of skin left by someone slipping through? But if injured, wouldn't they have gone for help?

Unless they weren't supposed to be there. Trespass. The first word on the crossword puzzle. Surely not . . .

Suddenly her appetite for lunch waned. "You two head on back, I think I will have a look around for a bit."

Betty Sue hissed near her ear. "Wanda, George said not to disturb the scene."

A grin slid up one side of Evelyn's mouth. "But you aren't, are you. You are looking for a trail. You want to know the direction in which the girl or woman came."

Wanda winked. "Exactly."

"Isn't it obvious?" Betty Sue shifted her gaze between them. "The shoe was wedged in the riverbed toe down, meaning she headed across from up here."

Wanda swiveled to face her. "Not exactly, Betty Sue. She crossed here but we don't know how long she followed the brook before deciding to do that. And if her shoe slipped off her injured foot, why didn't she stop to retrieve it?"

Evelyn huffed. "Because she was in a hurry."

"Bingo. If we learn her direction, we might discover why she didn't stop."

"Wanda, this isn't Scrub Oak. Let the authorities handle it." Betty Sue's voice trembled with intent.

Wanda pressed her hand to her heart. "I wouldn't dream of interfering. George obviously knows what he's doing. He will get a team together. They will be concentrating on identifying the owner of the shoe. DNA tests, if local stores sell that type of sock, and all that."

"So, what are you thinking?" Evelyn narrowed her focus onto Wanda's face.

Wanda detected a shimmer of excitement in her eyes. "Wandering upstream a bit and follow that barbed wire fence across the brook. But I want to find a shallower crossing. I'm guessing our shoe wearer would have as well." She started angling down the bank to the north away from the waterfall.

Evelyn's footsteps followed.

Above the current spilling over the rapids, she heard Betty Sue's sigh. "Guess we have a new scavenger hunt to begin. Wait for me."

CHAPTER 5

"Let's stay on the grass along the bottom of the slope if at all possible." Wanda weaved over the cypress roots hugging the narrow bank. "That way if there are any footprints, we won't disturb them."

Springtime in North Texas and Louisiana usually brought violent thunderstorms and downpours. But summertime typically remained hot and dry. The stream's depth showed signs of receding since the banks held mostly soft dirt, not mud. Wanda hoped a few telltale prints would be detectable but after fifteen minutes she stopped.

"We'd have seen something by now." Her expectations dampened, she motioned for them to head back the way they came.

"Maybe she waded in the stream, you know like the escaped convicts do in the movies to throw off their scent for the blood hounds." Evelyn loved to watch suspense and mystery shows. Westerns, too.

Betty Sue hitched her fists to her hips. "This isn't the nineteenth century."

Wanda held up her hand. "Wait, though. You may have a point, Ev. If her ankles were cut and hurting, the cool stream may have given her relief. Maybe she thought the water would stop the bleeding."

Betty Sue scrunched her nose. "And start an infection?" She pointed to some green moss clinging to the cypress trunks where the water's edge lapped.

"On the contrary, many ancient cultures used peat moss to stop bleeding and for medicinal purposes." Wanda grinned. "I learned that in Girl Scouts."

"Really." Evelyn harumphed. "Good to know."

Wanda laughed. "Though I have no idea why that tidbit surfaced in my mind just now. Usually, I can't recall where I laid my car keys."

Her two friends snickered in agreement. What sixty-something person didn't have mild memory issues? It's a topic many avoided in polite company though, lest people immediately think the "a" word—Alzheimer's.

The three trudged on in silence for several minutes. Wanda's back began to tell her it didn't want her bent over anymore. She stretched with a groan. "This is futile."

Evelyn agreed. "Good effort though. At least we can surmise she didn't come along the bank from the retreat center."

"True. Process of elimination. Let's head back before all the lunch is gone. Hot chicken salad sounded intriguing. Either of you ever have it?"

Her friends shook their heads.

The three returned to the chatter of happy women glad to have a break from their ordinary lives.

The carved-out watermelon, which had contained the fruit salad, appeared to be almost empty. Wanda forfeited her portion to Betty Sue. Evelyn had never been a big fruit eater.

After scooping some of the hot chicken salad onto a bed of lettuce and grabbing a yeast roll, Wanda followed her friends to a table where Martha and Rachel sat. The two already had dug into slices of grapefruit pie.

"You should try this, it is marvelous." Martha pointed with her fork. "And I am not always a fan of grapefruit."

The compliment made Rachel's eyes twinkle. "My mother's recipe. She grew up in the Texas Valley near McAllen. Only use ruby red grapefruit. It's sweeter and has much more flavor." Then she glanced up at the three joining them. "Oh, there you are. We wondered where you had wandered off to."

Inside her pleasantry lingered a question, at least to Wanda. She decided to ease the woman's mind. "We strolled upstream a bit before finding the path back. The bubbling current is so peaceful, and the cypress trees are magnificent. Reminds me of church camp in the Texas Hill Country back in the day."

Her answer satisfied the caretaker, or so Wanda surmised from the softening of Rachel's smile.

"You should take a short ride northeast of Monroe to the Chemin-a-Haut State Park. It has one of the biggest and most unique cypress trees in the state. One, nicknamed the Castle Tree, has a natural tunnel between the giant roots large enough to kayak through. They believe it is close to 1,000 years old." Rachel sat back, her grin showing she relished their astonished reactions.

"Wow. I definitely want to see that if we have time. When does the retreat end on Sunday?" Wanda glanced at Martha. Then she caught herself. "Not that I want to leave. This is a wonderful event."

Martha gave her a short laugh. "I understand. We end right after a short meeting following breakfast, so by eleven at the latest. You are, what? About a five-hour drive away from home? It might well be worth the two-hour diversion. You'd still be back in your town before dark. I can show you on the map where the state park is."

"Thanks." Wanda smiled. Not a big kayaker, but

such an old tree would be interesting to view.

Betty Sue put a forkful of chicken salad in her mouth and rolled her eyes. "This is marvelous. Definitely want the recipe!"

"All the recipes for the meals served during the retreat are available in the West Monroe Women's Auxiliary's cookbook. They are only ten dollars." Martha patted Betty Sue's arm. "Just let me know if you want one. I have quite a few in my trunk."

"Oh, I definitely do."

"Be sure to get a slice of pie, too." Martha wiped her mouth and excused herself from the table.

Her exit gave Wanda a chance to query Rachel. "So, tell me about your husband's career. My nephew is a police officer and is considering becoming a detective in a few more years."

Rachel took a sip of water then responded. "George was in naval intelligence so when he'd put in his twenty and retired, we moved here to be closer to my parents. He got his master's in criminal forensics at the LSU campus in Shreveport. Then he got a position at the Northern Louisiana Criminalistics Laboratory there. He retired three years ago from that job when we inherited this property."

Evelyn's eyes widened. "No kidding. Wow."

Wanda didn't try to hide her impressive reaction either. "Well, no wonder you called him to come take a look. I'm sure he'll get to the bottom of this in no time."

The owner shrugged as her eyes clouded over. Evidently, Rachel McDavid didn't share their enthusiasm in her husband's previous line of work.

Wanda glanced at Evelyn who raised her eyebrows and then continued to devour her lunch.

There had to be a way to speak further with the man. Could they stop up their toilet? Maybe not the best idea. A small fire in the kitchen as she helped prepare the evening meal might work. Then again . . . probably not. She'd had enough of soot-filled kitchens lately.

Wanda decided she'd think of some reason though. She had to find out more about that bloody sock. Every ounce of her sinew told her so.

But first, she wanted to grab one of the last pieces of pie.

HOT CHICKEN SALAD

This is a wonderful dish to serve to ladies on a retreat, or for a luncheon. Todd likes it, too, but he never revealed that fact to anyone except Wanda.

Ingredients:

- 3 cups cooked chicken breasts, shredded with a fork
- 2 cups finely diced raw celery
- ½ cup of toasted almond slivers
- ¾ teaspoon sea salt
- 3 teaspoons of grated yellow onion – Or you can use dehydrated onion flakes that have been soaked for a few minutes in tepid tap water then drained.
- 2 Tablespoons of lemon juice
- 1 ½ cups of mayonnaise – I like Blue Plate or Dukes for a good Southern flavor.
- 2 cups of shredded mild cheddar cheese
- One single serving bag of regular potato chips, not ruffled.

Directions:

1. Preheat oven to 350° F.
2. Lightly grease an oven-safe 9x14x2 glass casserole pan.

3. In a large bowl, blend together the mayonnaise, lemon juice and sea salt into a sauce with a spatula.

4. Add the veggies, almond slivers, and chicken.

5. Mix all of the ingredients together and spread evenly in the casserole pan.

6. Cover evenly with six ounces of shredded mild cheddar cheese, or a cheese blend.

7. Crush by massaging the bag of potato chips and sprinkle them on top.

Note: Betty Sue tried it with BBQ flavored chips and the casserole turned out okay. If you want to experiment with sour cream onion or jalapeno flavored ones, go for it. Just make sure the potato chips are not the thicker ruffled type. They get soggy.

8. Bake for twelve-fifteen minutes.

9. Spoon onto green leaf or Boston lettuce boats with a sprig of Italian parsley for garnish.

10. Makes 5-6 servings.

For fifteen ladies plus the speaker and host, we tripled the recipe and made four casseroles, just in case some might want seconds. Good thing—several did!

Chapter 6

Wanda couldn't keep her attention on the speaker, even after having a cup of coffee with her pie. She wanted to stand up and say, "Excuse me. Anyone lose a black sneaker with a bloody sock trimmed in pink apples?" But of course, that wouldn't do anything but produce negative vibes from the speaker and the other participants. Or start a mild panic.

She decided to sit on one of the large cushions so she would be able to glance at people's feet. She'd figure how to get up off the thing later. Or maybe she'd sleep there.

Martha clapped her hands to gain everyone's attention. Wanda perked up thinking she might ask them about the footwear. But she didn't.

"The winners of the crossword scavenger hunt are . . ." Martha paused for effect and wiggled her eyebrows.

Several ladies drummed the palms of their hands on the coffee table or their own knees.

"Room Three!"

Three ladies squealed and hugged while the rest mildly clapped.

From her vantage point, Wanda nonchalantly let her gaze land on ankles. None seemed bandaged. In fact, many of the ladies wore sandals. Three wore white tennis shoes, and two had kicked off their flip-flops.

The speaker came forward, wearing flats with no stockings unless they were those footies that only covered the bottom of the foot. She began the afternoon session with a prayer and then proceeded into her Power Point presentation.

"Grace could stand for goodness, reigned above, comes evenly." She pointed at each letter as she spoke, so they all got the anacronym. "Does anyone want to elaborate why God doles out His grace evenly? Or does He?"

One of the ladies answered the question in a rather lengthy reply, one Wanda had not paid attention to at all.

"Okay. By that you mean God doesn't play favorites, right? He extends grace to all of us." Mary Jane responded to the attendee, who nodded. "Let's explore that a bit. Does God give grace to everyone or just believers?"

That started a lively discussion. From the body language behind the professional smile, Wanda wondered if Mary Jane regretted bringing that topic up at all.

Evelyn offered her response with a tone of absolutism. She'd never known Evelyn to venture into shades of gray. With her, things were always black or white, yes or no. A woman of solid convictions, though sometimes a bit stubborn in her opinions, Wanda always admired her friend for standing her ground.

Betty Sue tended to waffle, seeing the best in each response, giving everyone validation, and affirming their right to their opinion whether it happened to be the same as hers or not. Her attitude came from years of teaching fourth and fifth graders, which had made her very popular with her students.

"You're awfully quiet." She leaned forward as she whispered into Wanda's ear since she sat on the couch behind her. "Mind back at the brook?"

Wanda chuckled. "You know me all too well."

Thank goodness the speaker announced the afternoon session over and free time would last for the next two hours, so everyone could either enjoy the sunshine, or have a nice nap. Several ladies must have preferred the second suggestion because they padded upstairs to their rooms.

A tall, dark-haired lady with a bird's nose asked if anyone wanted to start a game of Bridge, and immediately received three yeses. They headed for the card tables on the porch. Diehards!

Wanda rocked back and forth in an effort to rise from her cushion. She decided to slide onto her knees and then slowly raise up with a hand on the sofa arm behind her. Evelyn reached a hand down, and she took it as well.

"Why in the world did you choose to sit there on the floor?" Evelyn pulled Wanda's arm.

"Simple. Ankle observation." Wanda grunted as she stood upright. Success.

"Of all things." Betty Sue clucked. "I guess you are headed back to the scene of the crime?"

"What crime?" A white-haired lady named Olga Westheimer widened her robin egg blue eyes.

"Figure of speech. Nothing more." Betty Sue pressed her lips together.

"Oh." Olga's face drooped. "I love a good mystery. I thought perhaps it might have something to do with that shoe in the creek bed."

The three friends from Scrub Oak exchanged glances.

"You're wondering how I know, right? I heard Rachel and Martha discussing it as they unloaded the pies. I may seem the quiet wallflower, but I am very observant." She leaned back a bit and crossed her arms. "For example, I noticed you—" she stopped to read Wanda's name lanyard— "Er, Wanda from Scrub Oak, glancing at everyone's feet. Checking their footwear perhaps?"

Wanda sputtered and extended her hand. "Yes, as a matter of fact. Wanda Warner, and these are my friends, Betty Sue, and Evelyn. We're from a small town in North Texas about an hour southwest of Fort Worth."

"You've travelled a ways, haven't you? Olga Westheimer from Haughton just outside of Shreveport. Retired teacher, but my late husband was a private investigator and wrote whodunnits."

Evelyn gasped. "Stefan Westheimer? I love his books. Especially *Down and Deadly*." Evelyn had collected three bookshelves worth of cozy mysteries and crime novels over the years. Wanda didn't dare ask how many she'd downloaded into her e-reader. But she knew she'd been reading several of The Visitor Mysteries, a recent series of novellas by seven suspense and mystery authors.

Olga's cheeks grew pinker. "He especially loved writing that one, Evelyn. Spent a week on a duck farm doing research." Her eyes flitted to the side as if momentarily caught in a memory. Being widows, Betty Sue, Wanda, and Evelyn shared a sweet smile. They understood all too well how bittersweet recollections could be.

"Care to join us?" With immediate acceptance in the circle, Wanda pulled Olga out of the line of traffic and outside to the front porch. Betty Sue and Evelyn followed close behind.

"Absolutely. Are you headed back to the waterfall?"

"No. We have already scoped the bank. I wanted to follow the fence line to see if perhaps some of the barbed wire had tuffs of sock on it. Or flesh."

Wanda noticed Betty Sue shudder and make a face as if she'd smelled rancid milk.

Olga tapped her temple. "Smart. Those steel shards can definitely cut. Where do we begin?"

Wanda eyed the property. "Well, I guess we could split up and head in four different directions."

"Or start at the entry gate and then head off in pairs along the boundary. We'd eventually meet up again, yes?"

Wanda liked how Olga's mind worked. "Sounds good to me. Agreed?" She glanced at Betty Sue and Evelyn who both shrugged.

As the foursome strolled down the dirt and gravel road, Wanda pumped Olga for more information. "Did they say anything else?"

"Martha and Rachel? Not really. Just that someone named George decided not to contact the authorities."

That made Wanda jolt. "Why on earth not?"

"Didn't elaborate. In fact, Martha seemed a tad relieved."

"Really. Hmm."

Wanda chewed the inside of her lower lip. Hadn't George almost admitted the stains were indicative of someone being restrained? Wouldn't that hint of foul play?

She didn't have experience in forensics, but something didn't fit. Why had he decided not to pursue the issue? Could it have something to do with his grandson's graduation lock-in a few weeks back?

Julie B Cosgrove

CHAPTER 7

Evelyn's eyes pleaded to go with Olga, though Wanda would have liked the chance to chat with their new companion a bit more. To appease her neighbor, Wanda suggested they go left, and she and Betty Sue would take the fence to the right.

"What do you think of her?" Betty Sue kept her eyes to the bottom rung of barbed wire.

"Olga? Seems nice. Inquisitive, though." Wanda continued to check the tufts of grass with a stick. "Why?"

"Well, we didn't notice her by the stream so how did she know about the shoe?"

Wanda stopped. "She said she overheard Martha and Rachel talking."

"I suppose."

Betty Sue's voice ended in a lilt. Wanda had known

her long enough to know it meant she thought of something else but didn't quite decide whether to or not to say it. "Spit it out. What are you thinking?"

"Well, I don't recall her being in the group last evening during the icebreakers when we all introduced ourselves. Or this morning at breakfast. She seems the type of person who stands out in a crowd even though she called herself a wallflower. So, when did she arrive?"

Wanda stopped and stared at her friend. "You're right. If she had been here all along, Ev would have recognized the last name on her lanyard and made a beeline to her instantly. I mean considering who her late husband was."

"True. I guess maybe she could have come this morning. She doesn't live that far away."

"I wish we could determine how long that shoe has been in the stream. My guess would be not that long but with such little rain in the past few weeks, it is hard to say." Wanda sighed and continued to poke the tufts near the fence posts.

"Could the blood be from a snake bite, or an animal attack like a raccoon or skunk?"

"Good question, Betty Sue. But something George said keeps rattling around in my grey cells. Why would she—we assume it's a she from the pink apples stitched into the sock cuff and the narrowness of the shoe—not stop and try to loosen her shoe from the rocks?"

"True. And why would her sock come off?"

Her response halted Wanda again. "That's an even better question. Why indeed?"

She tilted her foot down and lifted her heel. The sock didn't slide. She jerked but the elastic band on the cuff held. "Maybe when the sock got wet from the current it expanded?"

Betty Sue crouched down to analyze Wanda's sock foot now dangling from her shoe. "Then wouldn't the blood have washed off?"

"I don't know. Maybe. Unless a lot had soaked inside." Tension began to strap Wanda's temples again. Two years ago, a mystery would have given her an adrenaline rush. Now, it seemed to follow her like a sinister shadow, and the desire to discover the reason became more of a rush to get it out of her life than excitement for pursuing the truth.

"Wanda, this is silly. There could be hundreds of reasons to leave a shoe deeply wedged in a river. Maybe she was in a canoe and slashed her leg on the rocks. The current became stronger, her friends called to her to hurry up, she jerked her foot out of her shoe, hopped in the canoe, and they slid over the small falls."

"Guess so. Did you realize the first clue's answer was trespass? I wonder if the McDavids allow hiking and canoeing through their lands. Another question to ask."

"Oh, good grief." Betty Sue slammed her hands to her sides. "Not every word puzzle leads to a crime, Wanda. Oh, why do I let you suck me into these things."

Wanda shrugged and wedged the heel of her shoe back on. "Could be a coincidence, I suppose." She glanced at the sky. Azure, not a cloud to be seen. No wonder her back felt overly warm. Her tongue slid around in her mouth as her mind thought of pitchers of ice-cold lemonade. Why had they not thought to bring bottles of water along with them?

"I'm thirsty. Is that stream along here somewhere?"

Betty Sue cocked her ear. "I think I hear it over there." She pointed to a line of dense greenery differing in color and pattern from the oaks and pines that cluttered the path. The cypress limbs reached to the sky as if to connect the waters in the heavens to the bubbling brook below. Almost as good as an oasis lined with palms in the desert.

The ladies scurried down the embankment and crouched down at the edge, cupping their hands in the cool waters and slurping.

"Please tell me we won't get parasites or amoebas inside us."

Wanda laughed. "Betty Sue. Really. Humans and animals have been drinking from this brook for centuries, maybe longer."

"I know." She wiped her mouth with the back of her hand. "But that was long before pollution, sewage dumping, and littering. We aren't that far from civilization."

Wanda's stomach flipped. "Thanks for the reminder." Then she snapped her fingers. "Wait a minute. You are absolutely correct. We need to find out what else is around here besides this retreat center. If the woman, girl . . . whoever, can't be identified as a guest here, then where did she come from?"

"You think George may know who she is and that's why he isn't contacting the authorities, don't you?"

"Perhaps. Though surely, he would have said so when he examined the sock. He gave me no indication that he did. Unless—"

"—He didn't think about until later. Which means he got caught up in the moment and then later on—"

"—Something or someone changed his mind." Wanda shot to her feet and glanced around. "He is bound to have neighbors. Maybe they would know something."

"Wanda, get real. How are we going to speak with them? We are here as guests on a retreat. To get away, relax, detox. Not solve a crime. And I now have serious doubts there has been one." Betty Sue puffed a long breath through her cheeks. Her jaw tightened as she rose from her squatted position by the edge of the stream.

Wanda stepped back. Rarely did her almost life-long friend get agitated. "You think I'm blowing this out of proportion."

"I think your curiosity is on overload. You aren't the neighborhood watch chairperson here in West Monroe."

Wanda grinned. "Brilliant idea. If they don't have a watch group out here, they need one. I plan to talk with Rachel about this at dinner. She is bound to show up while I'm on duty. Maybe if I can talk her into the idea, she will introduce me to other folk nearby and let me talk to them." She felt her brain cells sparking again. "It would be the perfect segue into asking if anyone has seen a girl with a hurt ankle hobbling around without a shoe."

Betty Sue threw her hands into the air. "I totally give up, Wanda Lee Warner. You are incorrigible." She stomped up the incline back towards the retreat center.

What's got into her?

CHAPTER 3

The group had an hour of free time left according to Wanda's watch, so she decided to continue on her search without Betty Sue. They'd patch things up later. They always did when their personalities clashed. A friendship lasting decades didn't shatter very easily.

Wanda waded across to the other side. She wandered that fence line for a while then realized she'd bypassed where the shoe had been discovered and ventured downstream from the waterfall. She heard it behind her. Unless there were two. She sort of doubted it.

Peering through the cypress-hugged shoreline, only woodlands with small patches of open glens extended as far as her eyes traveled. No other houses or outbuildings. Guess neighbors around here liked their privacy separated by several acres.

Where did the shoeless person originate? Had she come across those neighboring fields? Wanda sighed, almost deciding her efforts proved fruitless. Then something caught her attention. Squatting down with the trickling brook behind her, Wanda took a twig and poked at a white tuft hung one of the barbs. A squirrel in the cypress highway of limbs above her barked as if warning her of the evidence's presence. *Don't you dare touch, don't you dare touch, chitter, chitter chit.*

"Got it, little critter. Thanks." Wanda lifted the tuft with the small stick, but no blood or pink threads showed. The tiny piece of fabric could have come from anything.

She took several shots of the find with her phone anyway then decided to take a few more of the soft ground around the barbed wire. Two footprints indented the ground, presumably where the person had steadied his or her body to climb under or through the fencing. She knew her phone measured six inches because she had recently purchased a protective gel cover for it. She angled it over the imprint. At least an inch and a half hung out on top and bottom, so she guessed the size of shoe, which had left the mark, could easily be a nine.

Wanda took a cypress branch with a few sticky berries on it and wove it through the barbed wires, careful not to prick her skin. Then she reached up, twisted off another and wove it through in the opposite direction. There. X marked the spot.

She laid the piece back on the dirt and covered it with a stone. Then she took a photo of the scene up and down river to help identify it later.

Wanda rose and stared at the fence. Now what? Common sense told her to contact the authorities, but what would be the reason? George had a point, as had Betty Sue. Even a bloody sock did not indicate anything sinister had happened.

Even so, one unusual point remained. Why would anyone leave a shoe behind?

Only one reason—leaving the brook meant more to this person than retrieving her shoe. Either she was in a hurry to get away or someone hurried her away. Maybe she never cared for the footwear in the first place. Who knew for sure?

Maybe it gave her ankles blisters that had become bloody? Nah. In that case she'd have ditched the other one as well.

One other scenario chilled down Wanda's back. Had the wearer left her shoe wedged as a sign? "Hey, I came this way . . . in case someone is looking for me."

She swiveled around and peered down the current from the waterfall and then back upstream. Could the other shoe be nearby?

Satisfied she could locate the evidence again through her photos and the marking, Wanda wandered back toward the waterfall all the while shifting her eyes from the bank to the water. Though a bit murky, the shallows allowed her to make out the riverbed fairly easily. No black shoe-shaped object or white sock could be found.

She stopped, cupped a few more sips of water to quench her thirst and wiped her mouth with the hem of her T-shirt. Raising up, she scanned the banks and the waterfall once more. The absence of the other sneaker meant the owner might still be wearing it. But why?

What possible scenario would exist if foul play had not been involved. She mulled over Betty Sue's idea of getting into a canoe that had picked up speed down the waterfall. She had to admit it as a possibility, but if so, then the events were recent, as in today. Otherwise, wouldn't the group have already returned? Of course, they would've.

They would have hired or acquired the canoe upstream and gone for a trek. That meant they would return the way they came unless they'd arranged for another person to meet them downstream at their destination.

Even so, the girl would have insisted they come back for the shoe, right?

Unless she couldn't for some reason.

That realization sent another cold creep up Wanda's spine. She reached into her jeans pocket and pulled out her phone again. Three bars. Good.

The phone rang four times then clicked on the connection. Success!

"Hello, Todd?"

"I can't answer my phone right now so leave me a message. If urgent, call the Scrub Oak PD at—"

Wanda didn't listen to the rest. She clicked off without leaving a voicemail response. Dumb idea anyway. What could her nephew do in Texas when she stood on the bank of a brook in the woodlands of northern Louisiana? Hardly his jurisdiction.

The smart thing would be to get in touch with George. Or not. Something about the man hit her the wrong way, though she couldn't pinpoint what at the moment. More of an inkling. Woman's intuition? Maybe, a nudge from the Holy Spirit?

On the other hand, perhaps the man simply felt uncomfortable surrounded by a gaggle of women. A scientist more at ease among bubbling test tubes, laboratory rats, and microscopes than human beings. A possibility. Should she, as they learned so far at the retreat, show him a bit of grace and give him the benefit of the doubt? Probably.

She shrugged and headed back upstream.

Then someone yelled out her name. Shading her eyes from the afternoon sun, Wanda turned back and noticed Evelyn's green and white diagonally striped shirt on her tall, thin body. It reminded Wanda of an ecologically conscious barber pole. She both admired and envied her friend's ability to eat whatever she wanted and never gain a pound.

Their new acquaintance, Olga, followed closely behind. The two hugged the shoreline on the retreat side of the brook. Evelyn began speaking in rapid tones as they came even with Wanda, still walking on the other side.

"Hey. Guess what? We found something!"

In Olga's raised fingers dangled a white sock with pink apples on the cuff.

CHAPTER 9

Wanda almost felt giddy about her friends finding the matching sock. Would that be wrong? Doing so did make a case for the girl missing more than her footwear. Did it also suggest foul play enough to call the authorities?

"Where did you . . .?"

Olga twisted around and pointed behind them. "Down there. At the edge of the creek where the glen drops off."

"So, well past the waterfall."

"That's right." Olga grinned. "It had hooked onto a low hanging branch. I had to hold Evelyn's legs as she stretched across the bank over the water to retrieve it."

Well, that explains the dirty splotches on the front of Ev's green striped shirt. "No shoe?"

Evelyn glanced at the ground. "No shoe." Then her

gaze raised to meet Wanda's. "But no blood either. That's good, right?"

Wanda chuckled. "I guess. At least we know whoever lost these socks had two feet."

"Unless she had only one foot, which became injured, so her sock became bloody and then she tried to put on the spare, but it got snagged, so . . ." Evelyn moved her hands back and forth as if to erase the thought. "Never mind."

All three laughed.

A blush covered Evelyn's cheeks. "Where is Betty Sue? I thought you two searched together."

Wanda held up a finger and hopped rock to rock across the stream to their side. Then she answered. "She got kinda huffy. Felt I should forget the whole thing and enjoy the retreat instead."

"Oh." Evelyn pressed her lips together as if holding back any comment.

"Do you think I should?"

Neither lady said otherwise, which Wanda took as a yes. She reached for the sock then thought better of it in case modern forensics could retrieve fingerprints from knitted fabric. She recalled a TV crime show she and Evelyn watched where they gleaned DNA off of a guy's shirt. "Um, maybe we should bag that or something?"

"Good point." Olga patted her pockets. "With what,

though?"

Evelyn pulled her cell phone from its protective pouch she had clipped to her shorts' waistband. "This work?"

"Perfect. Great thinking, Ev." Wanda held it open as Olga slipped the sock inside and then stuffed it down with a stick. "Let's get back before they miss us."

The three wandered back to the retreat center in silence. Wanda mulled things over with each stride.

Tell George? Yes, no. Yes, no.

Call Todd and ask for his advice? Yes, no.

Call Mason and Vicki at the newspaper and have them search the newswires for missing women in this area. Hmm. Maybe.

"Ladies, you go on ahead. I will be there shortly." She dashed around the parking lot and pulled out her phone. Good. Four bars. She phoned the *Oakmont County Gazette*, tapping her nails on the back of the phone until she heard it connect. Jake Overby, the summer intern who filled in since Vicki had her hands full with the newborn Ian, answered.

"Jake, it's Wanda Warner. The one who produces the word puzzles?" She waited for his response then continued. "Well, I have sort of a puzzle here. Is Mason around?"

"Nope. 'Fraid not. He's at the City Council Meeting."

"Oh, of course. Well, can you have him call me?" She went on to briefly explain their discovery and what she needed. She knew the budding reporter's curiosity would be working overtime if she didn't.

"Wow. That's kinda cool, Mrs. W. I understand you are notorious for helping solve local crimes, and now you might have one in Louisiana?"

The admiration in his voice made her cheeks warm. She stuttered. "Not certain yet. Any help y'all can offer—"

"Yes, ma'am. I will let Mason know as soon as he walks in the door."

Wanda could tell from his enthusiasm he wanted marching orders, but she would not be the one to give them. That would be Mason's call as the Editor in Chief. "Thanks, Jake. Cell coverage is a bit spotty out here so feel free to leave a text message."

"Will do. Later."

Satisfied something would be happening while she listened more about grace, she sent up a prayer that if God had placed her here for a reason, He would provide confirmation. Perhaps then she'd speak with George.

As she entered the building, Martha cornered her. "Just a reminder since you are a number three. We are asking the dinner crew to arrive in the kitchen at 5:30, okay? Tonight, we are serving battered fish fillets and peanut rice pilaf with honey ginger veggies. Chocolate icebox pie for dessert, but Rachel has already purchased three of them so no worries about that. Even so, all hands on deck."

She wiggled her eyebrows and shuffled away.

Wanda had never heard of honey ginger vegetables, but the description sent a small grumble through her midsection. She patted her waist. "Very well, tummy. A small snack is in order perhaps, but not enough to ruin my appetite."

She grabbed a muffin cup of trail mix and an iced tea from the refreshment table and then took her place in the living room, this time on one of the sofas.

Betty Sue scooted over for her and smiled. "Sorry I got huffy."

"I understand. You organized Ev and me to come and there we go, off on a bunny trail." She squeezed her old friend's hand. "By the way, Ev and Olga found the other sock."

Wanda left the statement dangling in Betty Sue's mind—the way the sock had from Olga's fingertips—and faced forward, her attention on the leader calling them to prayer.

PEANUT PILAF AND HONEY GINGER VEGGIES

Several decades ago, Martha found this recipe in a magazine and served this with ham slices to her husband. He loved it. Later, whenever asked to bring a side dish he'd suggest she make it. She usually returned home with a scraped-clean dish. The ladies on the retreat all wanted the recipe so Wanda figured you would as well.

Note: Make this dish in two steps.

Peanut Pilaf
Ingredients:
- 2 Tablespoons – equals ¼ stick – of butter
- 1 medium yellow or white onion, finely chopped, or ½ cup frozen chopped onion pieces
- 1 chicken flavored bouillon cube
- 1 teaspoon sea salt
- 1 ½ cups of long-grain rice
- 1 10 ounces package of frozen peas
- ½ of a 12 ounce can salted, skin-peeled peanuts – not dry roasted. You can remove the red skins by rubbing the peanuts between your fingers.

Directions:
1. Melt butter into a four-quart saucepan over medium heat then sauté the chopped onions until clear and tender. If frozen, be careful or they may "spit" and burn your hand.
2. Stir in 3 cups of water, bouillon, and salt and

raise to high heat until a rolling boil, stirring occasionally to avoid any sticking to the bottom of the saucepot.

3. Stir in rice, reduce to low heat, and cover for about twenty minutes until rice is tender and most of the water absorbed.

4. Gently stir in frozen peas with a spoon or spatula to keep from breaking up the rice kernels. Then remove from heat once heated through and fold in peanuts.

Honey Ginger Veggies
Ingredients:

- 2 tablespoons of olive or avocado oil – I prefer avocado.
- 2 teaspoons minced fresh gingerroot
- 2 medium yellow squash chopped into bite-sized chunks.
- 2 medium green peppers chopped finely, or ½ package of frozen peppers – For added color you can use one red and one green.
- ¾ pound fresh mushrooms
- 1 ¼ teaspoons sea salt
- 1 tablespoon lemon juice
- 1 tablespoon of honey

Note: You can add a pint of halved cherry tomatoes if you wish. Betty Sue is allergic, so I usually don't.

Directions:

1. While the rice pilaf is simmering, sauté the ginger in the oil in a large skillet until a light golden brown. Enjoy the aroma! It will clear your sinuses.
2. Then stir in the peppers and squash and cook for five minutes until heated through and slightly tender, stirring often to ensure even cooking.
3. Add in the mushrooms and salt, continuing to stir until well blended.
4. Remove from heat and add to the rice pilaf.
5. Mix together the honey and lemon juice and fold it into the mixture.
6. Spoon onto a platter and serve hot.

Makes 6 servings (530 calories).

CHAPTER 10

Before she excused herself to help prepare dinner, Wanda felt the nudge to apologize to Betty Sue. She leaned to whisper near her ear.

"I understand where you came from, Betty Sue. Trust me, I hate that crimes seem to find me, but once they do, it is as if I've been assigned to help solve them. Otherwise, why would I basically be tripping over them in my path?"

"I see your point." She let out a sigh. "I guess I became disappointed because I wanted this to be a meaningful, devotional, and relaxing weekend with my dearest friends. And now this stupid sock has ruined it."

Wanda side-hugged her. "Make that two stupid socks and one stupid shoe."

They both giggled. The air cleared. Evelyn and Olga glanced over at them.

"What's up?" Evelyn's eyes darted between them.

Wanda often wondered if her neighbor felt left out since she had only known her for ten or so years while Betty Sue and Wanda had met in elementary school. "Filling Betty Sue in on your discovery. I left a message for Mason, too. I thought perhaps he could check the newswires for any missing girls or young women. You know, like those Amber Alerts."

"Why young?" Betty Sue knitted her brow.

"Know any women over thirty who would wear pink apples?"

"Well . . ."

Wanda threw her hands up "Never mind. I have to get into the kitchen. Here is a hint. Rice pilaf with peanut and honey ginger veggies." She slid her tongue over her lips and winked.

Evelyn scrunched her nose.

As Wanda chopped the squash and peppers, she heard her phone vibrate. She held it up to Martha and mouthed it must be important. Then she slid out the back door and sat on the outside stairs leading up to the door by their bedroom.

"Hey, Mason. Got my message?"

"Yeah. But, um, it sounded a bit bizarre, so I thought I'd call and make sure Jake got it correctly."

She let off a nervous chuckle. "Then he did. The landowner is a retired forensic scientist, and he played it all down, but he doesn't know we found the second sock."

"Bloody?"

"Nope. Clean. Well sort of. Definitely worn."

"I see."

Did he?

"So . . ." He paused. "You wanted to know about any reports of missing girls in that area, right?"

"Yep. Any news?" She cringed. "No pun intended."

"Ha, ha."

Wanda smiled. She really liked Mason. He and Todd had known each other in school, and he'd always been honest and hardworking. Now a caring father with a growing readership after taking over his father-in-law's newspaper and going digital with it, Mason had the world in his grip. Well, he knew he didn't—God did, and that perhaps made the difference.

His voice called her mind back to the conversation. "Yes, as a matter of fact there is an Amber Alert out for sixteen-year-old Sandie Hart." He scoffed. "Bet she is off with a boy."

Wanda didn't comment. "Where is she from?"

"West Monroe. Last seen at Chenreie Lake Park on Thursday. That isn't far from your location. About ten miles south."

The phone shook in Wanda's hand. "Details?"

"Sketchy. She is five-six, long blonde hair, blue

eyes, and weighs about one hundred-twenty pounds. She went hiking with a crowd from her high school but somehow got lost."

"Why an Amber Alert?" Usually, they were issued when minors went missing and a kidnapping by someone at least three years older seemed possible. At least, so Wanda understood.

"Her best friend found her pink sweater in the bushes half covered in leaves." Mason's chair thunked, which meant he must be leaning back in it. Obviously, Vickie was not there. She hated it when he did that. Scraped the wall and made her worry he'd tumble out of it and leave her a widow.

"Wait. Pink?"

Thud. His chair evidently landed back onto all four legs. "Let me verify . . . yep, says here she has an affinity for pink."

Uh, oh. "Did it say what she wore at the time?"

"Cut-offs, pint tank top. Pink and white striped bikini underneath."

"No mention of socks or color of her shoes?"

He paused. Then his voice came back. "Nope. You say the tread reminded you of runners? If they were hiking, it might make sense she'd be wearing a pair like that."

"Mason, is there a way you can check to see if she owns a pair of pink apple socks without raising parental hopes or fears?"

His voice softened. "Let me see what I can do. I will text you later. Tell Betty Sue and Ev hi for me. Oh, and Wanda?"

Yeah?"

"Have fun. Relax and enjoy time away with your friends. And text me photos of you three for *The Gazette*. I hear you have nicknamed yourselves the sows?"

Small town gossip spread as quickly as water from a hose down a steep driveway. "Yeah. It's a joke. Scrub Oak Widows Society."

"Cute." He hung up.

Oh, brother. No way she'd text him any pictures. Betty Sue and Evelyn would kill her if she did, and Hazel Parks and Beverly Newby back home might get their feelings ruffled that they had not been invited.

Wanda slid back into the kitchen and ignored Martha's glare. She returned to chopping the veggies then helped peel the red skin from the peanuts.

All through dinner her eyes kept wandering to the blackened phone screen she discreetly kept in her lap since they were supposed to not rely on electronic devices for entertainment.

She decided to keep her conversation with Mason to herself, for now.

Julie B Cosgrove

CHAPTER II

The next morning Wanda awoke to her phone buzzing. Mason.

She tiptoed out of the room, so as to not disturb Betty Sue and Evelyn, and answered in a whisper, knowing hallways carry sounds. "Hey, hang on and let me go outside where the reception is better."

In the middle of the hall, a short exit opened up to a balcony overlooking the pond. Rocking chairs dotted the expanse, and already three women sat watching the sunrise as they hugged mugs of coffee. Not much privacy there. She went out the side door near their room and crouched onto the top step of the stairs that led down to the kitchen stoop. "Okay. Whatcha got?"

"I've sorta talked with the Shreveport police."

Wanda sucked in a breath. "I really hadn't wanted you to contact the authorities. Not yet."

"I know, but as you said last night, we didn't want to stir up the parents, so, um . . ." He seemed to trip over his apology. "I contacted a guy I know there in dispatch who has a niece who goes to school with Sandie Hart, and I trust him to keep things low key."

Mason's network of informants continued to astound her. The guy had a knack, that's for sure. Some folks in Scrub Oaks accused him of gold digging when he got his degree in journalism while courting Vickie, the only daughter of Tom Jacobs, owner of the *Oakmont Weekly Gazette*. She saw his achievement as an act of love as well as a savvy business move to secure his financial future as a husband and later on, a father. Mason already had a degree in business, so taking the periodical reins fit him to a T.

Why did people say that? What is a T anyway? She made a mental note to do an internet search on the answer. Back to things at hand . . . "It's fine. I trust your judgement. What did you find out?"

"I told him you had found some discarded socks and described them. He checked with his niece who confirmed that Sandie could own a pair matching the description, though she can't recall if Sandie actually did. She said appliques socks were popular this year. She knew several girls who got a pair for Valentine's Day."

"Great. Kids and their fashion trends." Wanda

sighed.

"Right." He paused for only a second. "But it might be enough of a lead to warrant notifying the police who are investigating her disappearance. Especially the blood-stained one. DNA and all that."

Wanda watched two buzzards circling overhead in the pinkish morning sky above the tree line. That gave her a bit of a start until she realized the birds searched well upstream from the location of the shoe, opposite of the direction where Ev and Olga had found the second sock. Besides, if the carcass they sought was larger than a squirrel, more of their feathered friends would be joining them for the banquet. "Okay, so who do I get in touch with?"

"Sergeant Mulligan. He is in charge of the case. I will text you his number."

"Thanks, Mason."

"Sure, but in the meantime, do you want Jake and I to do some background check on Sandie? Her digital footprint, and such? No pun intended."

Wanda snickered. "I'm sure the police are already doing that. But, why not? If you have time."

He laughed. "Well, since you are not here seeking out possible criminal activities, things are fairly dull around Scrub Oak at the moment."

She spit a raspberry sound into her phone. One of the women, who must be on the breakfast team, halted on the path to the kitchen below and gazed up at her with a questioning expression on her face.

Wanda waved and rose to go back inside. "Later, Mason. I will keep you posted at my end. My love to Vickie and little Ian."

"Thanks, and say a prayer he will start sleeping at night, okay? We're exhausted."

"He will, give it a few months."

"Guess we have no choice." Mason yawned into the receiver.

"You'll survive. God designed people to have babies when they're young for a reason. Except for Sarai and Elizabeth in the Bible, of course, but I imagine He took that in account and gave them some heavenly booster."

"I could use that!"

Wanda snickered as she hung up.

She slipped back down the hallway and cracked open the door to find Betty Sue up and bending over her suitcase. Ev's bed had already been made up. She must have gone down for breakfast prep.

"Where have you been?" Betty Sue lifted her attention from gathering her towel and toiletries.

"Talking with Mason out on the stairwell."

Betty Sue's eyes widened. "Mason is here?"

Wanda scrunched her eyebrows then realized the confusion came from her syntax. "No, I spoke with him on the phone as I sat on the stairs."

"Oh." She closed her suitcase. "Is everything all right?"

"Yes . . ." How much did she want to divulge? She hated to instigate another argument.

Betty Sue stared at her for a moment. "It's about the sock, right?"

"Yeah, it is. Do you want to know?"

"Sure. I mean I may as well. From the look in your eyes, it is important, right?"

"I'm afraid so. In fact, I need to call the police."

"Why?" Her question came out in a higher octave, almost a squeak.

Wanda breathed through her nose. Here goes . . . She spat it out as fast as she could. "A teenage girl from West Monroe named Sandie, who likes to wear pink and probably owns a pair of socks like the ones we found, went missing on Thursday."

"Mercy. That was day before yesterday." Betty Sue plopped onto her bed and clutched her hands between her knees. When she lifted her gaze, her eyes shimmered. "Do they expect foul play?"

Wanda came and sat next to her. "They may once I tell them what we've found."

"Oh, dear." She hung her head as if in prayer.

Wanda waited.

Betty Sue sniffed and opened her eyes. "I am sorry

I got upset. I should know by now to trust your instincts." She grabbed Wanda's hand and squeezed it. "You better make the call."

"Right." Wanda pulled up the number Mason had texted to her and highlighted it, telling her phone to connect her. By the Almighty's goodness, she actually got the call to go through.

After she had made her report she nodded. "I see. Okay."

"Well?" Betty Sue's eyes explored Wanda's face.

"They are sending an officer to retrieve the shoe and collect the sock from George. Is the other one still in Evelyn's phone pouch?"

"Not sure." She rose and took it from the bedside table. Lifting the flap and peering inside, she nodded.

"Good. I'll text the police that we have found the matching one. Then all we can do is get dressed and wait."

A wave of sadness and helplessness washed over her. She wished she could do more, such as find Sandie. Wanda gulped the emotions back and gathered her clothes to change into for the day.

CHAPTER 12

After she dressed, Wanda went in search of Martha to let her know the police would most likely be knocking on the door. She rehearsed how to explain without riling up too much emotion as she trudged down the stairs to the kitchen. She assumed Martha would be hovering there barking out commands like a drill sergeant. Okay, not a fair analogy. The woman definitely had excellent organizational talents, which is why she had been put in charge of the weekend events. By her fervor, Wanda knew she took her assignment seriously. Probably had spent weeks pulling it all together.

Wanda lifted her eyes and apologized to the heavens, then asked for the right words to say. Her prayer must have been heard because Martha's face only paled slightly when Wanda filled her in.

"Well, I better contact George, then. I imagine he will want to meet them here." She set down the broom from sweeping some spilled oatmeal flakes and sighed. "What on earth made you decide to search for the other sock?"

Wanda shrugged. "A gut feeling."

A wry smile slid over the retreat coordinator's lips. "Or divine intervention. This has happened to you before, hasn't it?"

"A few times." Wanda held her tongue. No sense in explaining all her sleuthing over the past few years that led to solving three murders, a drug ring, and a kidnapping.

Martha took her by the elbow. "We better inform Mary Jane as well and then make an announcement during breakfast, so the ladies are not shocked."

"Good idea." Wanda glanced to the right and saw Evelyn's eyebrows knit into the wrinkles across her forehead. She mouthed, "Explain later."

Evelyn gave her a wink and went back to whisking the eggs.

As the women gathered for prayer before hitting the breakfast line, Martha made an announcement. "Ladies, during the scavenger hunt yesterday, Team Five stumbled upon a shoe in the creek with a pink apples sock in it. Then they discovered the other sock further downstream. We have since learned it may belong to a teenage girl who has gone missing from Chenreie Lake Park, so the police are on their way to collect these items. There is nothing to worry about, but I suggest we pray for the girl, Sandie, to be found safe and sound."

Murmurs floated through the group. One lady mumbled a complaint about why the police didn't patrol the area better. Teenagers were up to all sorts of shenanigans—her word—up there every summer.

Mary Jane gave the group a terse smile. "Let's remember we are not to judge, but to show grace. And to pray. That is the way to win souls for Heaven. Now, let's bow our heads."

Breakfast was blessed, served, and thankfully consumed before the patrol cruiser's tires popped along the gravel road and stopped at the cabin.

Wanda, Olga, Betty Sue, and Evelyn met with Officer Mulligan outside to give their statements and hand over the evidence from Evelyn's purse pouch. George observed the exchange with narrowed eyes and a tight jaw as he held his contribution in an evidence bag. After handing it to Officer Mulligan, George walked him back to the police cruiser and spoke with him out of earshot.

"Wonder what that's all about?" Evelyn harumphed.

"The policeman probably knows him, or of him. He is the property owner after all. Anyway, it is out of our hands now." Wanda rubbed hers together for emphasis as if washing herself of the whole thing.

"Wanda Warner! You are letting this go without finding out what happened to that girl? That's not like you."

She gave Evelyn a wry grin. "I never indicated I would. Only that the evidence is now with the professionals to determine if they belong to her. We still do not know why she went missing, do we?"

Betty Sue rolled her eyes as Olga stared.

"But you plan to find out, right?" Evelyn rocked back with her eyes resembling an owl's round and alert ones.

"If I can. But only if it doesn't disturb the real reason we are here, right Betty Sue? The next session is about to start, I believe." Wanda turned and strutted back into the cabin.

But Wanda barely heard the talk by Mary Jane, and when they broke out into discussion groups, her mind kept slipping away from the conversation among the other women in her circle. She glanced out the window to the group where Evelyn had been assigned, seated on the grass. Their eyes met. Evelyn raised an eyebrow in her direction and then shifted her eyes toward the creek. Wanda nodded.

Wanda raised her hand. "I'm sorry. Nature is calling." Well, not a real lie, was it?

She rose and received a couple of sympathetic expressions. She went in the direction of the downstairs bathroom but then turned and tiptoed out the side door that faced the fields. Evelyn had already headed across the grass. She sprinted to catch up to her.

Evelyn nodded at her. "Are we playing hooky?"

"Perhaps, Ev. But these sessions are not mandatory, you know. We paid our money. It is up to us how much we wish to participate."

"Well, you know the only reason I came is because you and Betty Sue twisted my arm. I normally don't go in for these Kumbaya things."

Wanda couldn't help but laugh. "They have their purpose. We women need to get away and be together at times. Back in the day women did so more often. They had sewing and quilting bees, made jams and canned together, even did the washing at the brook in groups."

"True. Today we have social media. Guess it's not the same." Evelyn kicked a tuft of grass. "And this grace thing is worth thinking about. I just despise discussion groups. Always have."

"Hey, wait up!"

They turned to view Olga scurrying toward them. "I saw you two escaping and decided to follow, okay?" Her voice labored between short quick breaths.

"Sure. Glad for the company." Evelyn's face brightened. "By the way, what are we doing, Wanda?"

She chuckled. "Heck if I know. Going back to the scene and pondering. Maybe we will notice a twig snapped or some footprints we didn't see yesterday." Then she remembered. In her phone lay just that. And she hadn't told the policeman about it either. Where was her brain? After her friends found the other sock it didn't seem as important. She hoped so.

As they approached, they noticed a patrol car parked near the top of the embankment and heard men's voices.

"Uh, oh. We aren't the only ones with this idea." Wanda halted. Through the tree limbs she noticed the plaid on George's shirt as she gazed down the bank. "Why don't we head to the spot where you two found the second sock."

"Good plan." Olga pointed out the direction as the three stealthily moved away, trying to make their footfall as soft as possible.

When they arrived at the place, Wanda divulged her conversations with Mason and her finding the footprints and piece of fabric in the barbed wire.

"Wow, you have been busy. Remind me to consult

with you when I plot my novel." Olga gave her a head bob.

"You're gonna write one?" Evelyn's interest perked.

"After helping my late husband all those years research and develop plots, I thought I might as well carry on the legacy. Well, I've toyed with the idea for several months now, but this weekend has solidified my desire."

"Wonderful!" Evelyn clapped her hands together. "I have three bookshelves of whodunnits, and half a shelf is dedicated to your late hubby's books."

"Not to mention the collection of DVDs on crime dramas and mysteries from Agatha to Zed, including that new British series streaming now." Wanda winked. "This lady can tell you if a crime you are thinking of has been solved before in fiction and by whom."

"I am impressed." Olga whistled through her teeth. "So, between the three of us, with Mason researching back home in your town, discovering what happened should be fairly easy."

"We can only hope so, Olga." Wanda stepped over a high tuft of grass. "From my experience though, once we start peeling the onion, the more pungent layers emerge, making us recoil. What we thought might be true usually ends up being something else."

The three squatted down on the rocks near the creek

and scrutinized the surroundings.

"Why did the other sock end up here, about a quarter mile downstream?" Wanda almost whispered the question. She tilted her head toward the other two ladies' faces. "Dry or damp when you discovered it?"

Olga met her gaze. "Dry. For the most part. A tad bit damp around the toe and the cuff. Why?"

"Then it seems it may have once been wet, like its counterpart, but drip dried on the branch." Wanda squinted and shielded her eyes from the morning sun. "If only the toe had been damp, it could have been from the creek's current splashing up from the rocks. But the cuff was slightly wet as well? I gather that's how it had been hung, right?"

"Correct." Evelyn stood. "So, someone placed it there on purpose."

"And quite a while before you two discovered it. Maybe a day?"

"Not necessarily." Olga pointed to the limb. "That branch is in the shade now, but yesterday's afternoon sun shone onto the sock, which is why it caught my eye. Therefore—"

"It could have been left several hours earlier!" Evelyn's voice became almost giddy. "That establishes the time."

"Maybe." Wanda raised her finger. "Today is Saturday. I wonder when her friends noticed Sandie missing on Thursday, and exactly how far away this lake park is by foot."

"Or canoe." Olga pointed downstream where the brook forked into a large stream. "That's the North Cheniere Creek. It meanders to the southwest and dumps into the lake about two or so miles away."

"Wait." Wanda's brain kicked in overtime. "It would seem then she headed back to the lake, not away from it."

Evelyn snapped her fingers. "Which means she escaped her kidnappers and headed back to find her friends."

"If she'd been kidnapped. She could've decided to run off with a boyfriend then changed her mind." Wanda narrowed her eyes. "The question remains—"

"—Where is she now?" Olga nodded.

The three glanced around them as a breeze scooped up the coolness from the stream and swooshed it over their shoulders.

Why did Wanda suddenly feel as if they were being watched? And by whom? She glanced up the banks on both sides but didn't detect any movement. Even so . . .

Had George followed them and peered down on them? She wondered if he knew more than he let on about this whole mess. His grandson would be close to Sandie in age. Did he know her?

His wife, Rachel, seemed nice enough but

something about George didn't sit right in Wanda's gut. He downplayed finding the sock and shoe once he examined them. Then, today when he learned they'd found the second sock as they turned it over to the police, Wanda detected a twitch on his lip. Just before he hurried the policeman off to the side for an out-of-earshot chat.

A premonition of menace tingled her bones. She didn't know these folks. Were they trustworthy?

There seemed no tactful way to ask Martha her impression of George. Betty Sue always saw the best in people so asking her opinion wouldn't be fruitful either. Wanda could ask Evelyn or Olga but did that border on gossip? She sighed.

Perhaps Mason and Vicki could find out about him. Search the social media sites for comments from his colleagues and such. Though what anyone posted these days had to be taken with a boulder of salt, much less a grain, as the saying went.

She suspected George knew Sandie and recognized the sock as hers. She may have been a girlfriend of one of his grandson's buddies at the lock-in. Had his grandson dated her? Now there's a thought. But how could she find out? Casually start a conversation—Hey, George, did your grandson go the lake park with Sandie and her friends? Did you know she'd gone missing? Like he'd give her an answer.

"You seem deep in thought." Evelyn's voice penetrated her surmising. "Whatcha got churning up there?"

Wanda blinked. "Nothing. Really. Simply trying to piece this together for the most logical scenario. George's grandson seems to be similar in age so I wondered if he might have any insight. Maybe he knows these kids, Sandie in particular. So how do we get in touch with him?"

Olga clicked her fingers. "Hey, there is a guest book at the cabin. Long shot but maybe one of the boys signed it? At least we'd have a name. Maybe even a phone number or address."

Evelyn scrunched her nose "What good would that do us?"

"Well, these kids are all online chatting and tik-toking or whatever. We might be able to message one of them."

Wanda gave her a thumbs up. "Good thinking. Welcome to the SOWS. Scrub Oak Widows' Society. You are now an honorary member along with my good friend DiAne."

Olga laughed. "I'm honored." She swooped into a bow, with one hand out and one tucked to her waist.

Evelyn clapped.

The three headed back to the retreat center to take a good glance at the guest book. Who knew? One of the guys just might have thought it funky enough to sign his name.

CHAPTER 13

Sometimes God gives small serendipities. Sure enough, two of the boys had thought it cheesy enough to sign their names. One had even left his phone number in case any "hot chicks" decided to get in touch with him.

"Do we dare call?" Evelyn's eyelids stretched wide.

"Why not. I've lost thirty pounds, after all. I do look kinda hot even if I say so myself." Wanda pumped her hip then took out her cell phone from her pocket. She punched in the number but didn't hit the send button. "Better do this outside."

Betty Sue saw her. "Wanda? Where have y'all been?" Her tone smacked of finding truant kids.

"Do you want to know?" Wanda spit out the question then wished she hadn't. "I am sorry, Betty Sue. Forgive my tone. We have been sleuthing. Trying to find Sandie."

"Sandie? Oh, the missing girl. You think it's her sock and shoe?"

"And other sock. Yes."

Betty Sue's face grew serious. "Be careful, Wanda. You, too, Ev."

"We are." Evelyn answered, but not with a smile.

Wanda hated the tension building between her and her friends. "Betty Sue, I know you don't approve but we found the stuff. I am really worried that the girl is somewhere close by and may be injured."

Betty Sue's countenance softened. "I get it. I do. It's just . . ."

"You wanted us all to enjoy this retreat and now crime seems to have seeped in."

"Yes. It seems to find you like pet hair finds a freshly dry-cleaned skirt." Her lower lip protruded into a pout.

Wanda shrugged. "I agree. Maybe for a reason?"

Olga stood by, quiet as a librarian. Poor woman probably felt awkwardly out of place. Wanda turned to her. "Betty Sue and I have been friends since third grade. We speak our minds. It is the strength in our relationship."

That did it. Betty Sue's angst melted, and she side-hugged Wanda. "It's only that I care. I don't want you back in the hospital."

"That was a while back, and I am not being kidnapped in a van again. I promise." She thumped her chest. "Doc gave this old ticker a clean bill of health last visit."

Then something occurred to Wanda. Betty Sue's semi-beau, Fred, had been a high school principal for years. He may have connections. "Betty Sue, do you think Fred might know the high school principals in this area? Maybe he could help discover who her friends were and where she might be."

"Well, he might. I guess I could call and ask him. I am worried about her as well, you know."

"Great! And here are two boys that are friends of the caretaker's grandson, who is also in high school. I imagine here in the Monroe or West Monroe area." Wanda showed her the picture of the guest book she had snapped with her phone. "I'll text it to you."

"Okay, but they are about to serve lunch. You'll like it. I helped make it."

Knowing her dear friend's propensity for healthy foods, Wanda had her doubts. But her stomach did feel as if its needle edged to the E.

"Sounds good. Ladies, shall we?"

Evelyn and Olga nodded.

"What's on the menu?" Now that she thought about it, something did smell delicious.

"Cheeseburgers. George has been grilling them.

Isn't that sweet of him?" Betty Sue grinned.

"Oh? Sounds like a nice guy thing to do." Contriteness oozed up Wanda's chest. So not spying on her in the field overlooking the brook then. So, who did? She definitely had the intuition . . .

"And for the side, pineapple casserole. It's really good. Fattening, but good." Betty Sue's eyebrows wiggled. "Made with butter, sugar, Ritz crackers, and cheddar cheese."

"Yum." Wanda hurried her pace. No time to think about the calories that would go straight to her hips.

Betty Sue had been correct. Pineapple casserole could only be described in one word . . . scrumptious.

Evelyn forked it. "Never heard of such a thing. Tasty, though."

"Well, you eat apple pie with a slice of melting cheese. This is similar if you think about it." Wanda pointed at the portion on her plate before taking another bite.

They finished and left the table to wander outside by the pond for a post-feast stretch.

Wanda stopped and gazed across the shoreline to the tall trees. The blue sky, now dotted with fluffed white clouds, glided in the water's reflection. "This place really is nice."

"Glad you came, then?" Betty Sue nudged her.

Wanda snickered. "Yes. Thanks."

Evelyn patted her belly. "Food's wonderful, too."

Olga agreed. "One of the reasons I love these retreats. The food is always fabulous. A committee goes over the recipes and tries them out first."

Wanda turned to her. "You come often?"

"Uh, huh. Every year. Our church ladies come here because Martha is a life-long friend. She is one of our deacons."

"Evelyn is a deacon at her church, too." Betty Sue laid a hand on her friend's shoulder.

"Really? Good for you." Olga smiled. "George and Rachel are kind enough to offer the retreat center pro bono even though they go to a different church because Rachel and Martha do Meals on Wheels food prep together. That way, the proceeds from the retreat all go to food, the speaker, and the rest to our church's outreach program in Kenya."

Wanda cocked her head. "You know Rachel and George then?"

"Oh, yes. Somewhat. My late husband used to consult with George on his books to make sure the forensics were authentic."

"Have you met his grandson, then?"

"He has three. But yes. I'm sorry, I just now connected the dots. When you said sleepover, I was thinking about the ten-year-old, Franklin. The one who is a senior in high school is called Flex. Actually, his real name is Felix, but he hates being called that. He likes to work out, thus the nickname. He's on the wrestling team for West Monroe High." Olga set down her fork. "Just a minute. I think I kept the news article about them winning area." She scrolled through her phone.

Wanda waited as her new friend searched the entries saved on her phone. She glanced around the lawn and saw several other ladies who'd also chosen to ignore the no-devices rule. *Oh, how dependent we all are on our phones!* But to be fair, people used them to capture memories and they might have a Bible app downloaded.

"Why didn't I think of this earlier?" She clucked and slapped her temple. "My brain." Then she stopped scrolling. "Here we are. From the West Monroe newsletter last March."

Bingo. Under the photo the article listed all their names, including the two boys who had signed the guestbook. That meant at least a few of the team had attended the lock-in.

"Any of them go to your church?"

Olga nodded. "As a matter of fact, yes. This one does. Brad Feller. He sometimes brings Flex. I'll call his mother. We are on the hospitality committee together."

Wanda winked at Evelyn and Betty Sue. Brad Feller had been one of the signatures, the one looking for a hot chick. Yep, God's little serendipities.

PINEAPPLE CASSEROLE

Ingredients:

- 1 roll of Ritz crackers crushed into crumbles
- 1 stick of unsalted butter, cut into cubes and left at room temperature
- 2 20 oz cans of pineapple chunks, drained
- 1 cup sugar
- 5 tablespoons of flour
- 1 1/2 cup of grated Colby or medium cheddar cheese – I prefer medium. It is more flavorful.

Directions:

1. Preheat the oven to 350° F. Very lightly grease the sides and bottom of a Pyrex 9X12 pan with avocado oil, using a paper towel or your fingers.
2. Mix together the pineapple, sugar, and flour in a bowl. Then fold in the cheddar cheese until evenly coated. Spread evenly into the pan with a spatula.
3. In another bowl, cut together the butter cubes and crumbled crackers with a fork until well

blended and add it to the top of the pineapple mixture.

4. Bake for 30 minutes.

Makes 6 servings. Goes great with baked or fried chicken, hot dogs, or even fish sticks! A good potluck side dish, too. In fact, both Wanda and Betty Sue showed up with it at the last women's luncheon, which turned out okay because everyone wanted some.

CHAPTER 14

During their two-hour afternoon break, Wanda, Betty Sue, and Evelyn listened in on speaker mode while Olga phoned Brad. He answered the phone reluctantly, a question already dangling in his tone.

"Mrs. Westheimer? Can I help you?"

"We hope you can. Your mom gave me your cell phone number. You probably heard about Sandie Hart going missing."

"Um . . ."

"Do you know her? Who she hangs out with or who she is dating?"

"Why?" His tone remained guarded.

Betty Sue motioned to hand her the phone. Wanda whispered into Olga's ear that she had a way with students back in Scrub Oak.

Olga relinquished the phone with a shrug.

"Brad, my name is Betty Sue Simpson from Texas. You see, while on a scavenger hunt here at Flex's family cabin we found a black, ladies' athletic shoe and a pair of apple socks near the waterfall, and we wondered if they might belong to Sandie. If they do, it might help the authorities find her. But we didn't want to contact her parents and get them all upset, you know?"

"Yeah. That makes sense."

"Do you know of anyone we could speak with who might know? We're just concerned. No one is in trouble."

They heard him sigh. "Um . . . look. I'm not sure. I mean I know of her, but we don't hang out, ya know? But she did date Aiden for quite a while. Like since his sophomore year. He is on the wrestling team with me and Flex, so we were all at that cabin a few weeks ago."

"Aiden . . .?"

"Mulligan. A senior. A year older than me and Sandie. She called while we were up there and broke it off. Said she'd met some college guy. I don't know who. Aiden seemed really torn up about it. I mean, he punched a hole in the wall of his room. I helped him and Flex repair it though."

Betty Sue glanced at Wanda. From her expression Wanda sensed they wondered the same thing. An angry ex-boyfriend with a volatile temper spelled trouble. Did he kidnap her to keep her from seeing the college guy?

Wanda wrote down her question about Sandie's love of pink. Betty Sue read it and nodded, then asked Brad. "Listen, do you ever recall her wearing pink apple socks?"

"Well, yeah. Aiden gave them to her for Valentine's. Sandie's favorite snack is an apple. So he got them for her, along with a dozen pink roses and chocolates, of course."

"Have you spoken to Aiden in the past few days?"

"Um, why?" His tone became hesitant again.

"We'd like to speak with him. See if he could help us—"

"Look, I don't know who you ladies are, okay? I mean except for Mrs. Westheimer. But the cops already drilled Aiden. He didn't go to the lake on Thursday. He and Flex did something together. I went ziplining over the gators near Shreveport with two other guys, Blake and Wayne so I didn't go either. I have no idea what happened there."

Wanda mouthed "what?" to Olga and she nodded. She whispered back that kids around there zipline over the gators a lot. That gave Wanda the shivers. Why were teens so drawn to danger? Then she caught Betty Sue's voice and listened again.

"Never mind, then, Brad. We gave the socks to Flex's grandfather, and he gave them to the police. We simply wondered. No big deal. I hope they find Sandie safe and sound."

"Yeah, well. I wouldn't know. And I'm sure Aiden doesn't either." His breathing became short and quick. They had obviously irritated him, and he seemed ready to defend his friend at all costs.

Betty Sue sweetened her tone like four teaspoons of cane sugar in a glass of Southern tea. "Thank you so much for speaking to us. Glad you are there for Aiden and are such a good friend. Sounds like he needs it right now, so good for you."

"Um, sure. Okay. Bye."

Betty Sue handed the phone back to Olga. Then she turned to Wanda. "He is very defensive. Do you think he's lying?"

Olga harumphed. "You mean covering for Aiden?"

"You're the expert when it comes to teens." Wanda eyed Betty Sue. "You tell us."

She shook her curls. "Me? Not really. Fred would be, though. Oh, drat. I forgot to call him." Her face reddened. "I'm so sorry. Let me get my phone and do that now."

She dashed back inside the cabin.

Wanda turned to Evelyn. "Thoughts?"

"We now know those socks most likely belonged to a missing teenage girl who had recently broken up with a young man who is very physically fit. Plus he has a hair-trigger temper. And he is a friend of the forensic scientist's grandson." She counted her points out on her fingers. "My gut tells me those boys know a good deal more but are afraid to come forward because of George McDavid's connections and reputation. His grandson doesn't want to fall from grace."

Like a splash of cold water on a hot August day, a thought hit Wanda, as they sometimes do.

"Grace. Our topic. Why didn't we connect the dots?" She put both hands to her head as if holding it would keep her brain from spewing all of her ideas before she could cognitively categorize them. "Wait, I have to work this out."

She wandered over to a bench under a sprawling oak near the pond. Evelyn and Olga silently followed.

After a minute Wanda glanced up. "One of you go get the crossword puzzle from the scavenger hunt, please."

"I'll go get mine. It's folded up in my Bible." Olga dashed away.

Wanda gazed into Evelyn's face. "The crosswords led us to the waterfall where we found the bloody sock and shoe. One of the other clues was 'trespass.' Sandie may have been doing just that. And 'doe?' Well, I am still working on that." She brushed the thought away with her hand and sighed. "Could it be a coincidence, or did someone design the clues for us to find her things?"

"Nope, I doubt it's anything like that." Evelyn

crouched on the grass. "We had it wrong, remember? Martha told us the clue for pour meant the old water pump."

"True. Though the passage definitely said 'pour' not 'drip'." The idea began to fizzle like a sparkler on the Fourth of July, then it crackled as a new spark lit up again. "Unless . . . I wonder how Betty Sue found it."

"On her morning walk."

"Yes, but why did she head in that direction?"

Evelyn lifted one shoulder in response.

Wanda texted Betty Sue, figuring she might still be on the phone with Fred. Betty Sue often stayed on the phone with Fred these days. Their relationship certainly had budded into something sweet. For their sakes, Wanda hoped it would continue.

A few minutes later she got a ping. *I think Martha suggested it. I wanted a quiet place of solitude because something Mary Jane said Thursday evening hit a chord with me.*

Hmm. Wanda made a mental note and placed it with the other questions beginning to form in her brain. Not about Betty Sue. She knew her friend well enough to understand the woman always thought things through before reacting. One of the attributes Wanda admired most about her. In fact, it made Wanda glad that somebody got something out of this weekend. Come to think of it, that probably explained the reason for their spat earlier. She wanted Wanda to experience the same.

No, another tidbit tickled Wanda's thoughts like an unreachable itch in the middle of her back. Did Martha send her in that direction on purpose?

"Ev, do you recall any of the other clues?"

"Nope. You were the one studiously working them out."

Wanda leaned back. "Right. And I didn't get very far. I have an inkling they hold a clue for us, though. One I can't quite shake away."

"Uh, oh. Are you certain your brain doesn't naturally go there because word puzzles have led to crime solving in the past? This ain't Scrub Oak, my friend."

Wanda glanced at the cottonwood trees' white puffs softly meandering across the sky. A few landed in the pond and floated like teeny paper sailboats. "Possibly. I don't know. Let's wait and see when Olga comes back with the crossword sheet."

As if the thing would have some secret Nancy Drew code on it. Wanda could only wish.

Julie B Cosgrove

CHAPTER 15

Olga jogged back with the crossword sheet in her hand and gave it to Wanda.

"Here. My room didn't complete it, but we got to clue number four—from his fullness we have received grace upon grace, from John's first letter in the Bible. We figured fullness referred to our stomachs after breakfast and that led us to the kitchen where the pantry was stocked to the hilt."

"I don't recall that clue?" Wanda knitted her brow in concentration. Where would fullness fit into the puzzle? "Let me see that a second."

She scanned the paper and shook her head. The clue about a drip was there. The question stemmed from Proverbs 27:15. "A continual dripping on a rainy day and a quarrelsome wife are alike." The hint read: what we tend to do instead of showing our husbands or bosses grace.

"The clue about grace pouring. From the Psalms, right, Ev?"

"I think so. Yeah."

"I don't see it." Wanda felt a tingle in her bones. She raised her gaze to Evelyn's eyes.

"Uh, oh. I know that look, Wanda Warner. Your brain is spinning."

"Remember down by the creek when we explained the clue led us to the waterfall?"

"Yeah?"

"Martha said the clue had been drip, not poured. The pump dripped. That question is here on Olga's sheet, but it wasn't on ours as I recall."

Evelyn's eyes widened as she scanned the sheet. "Well, I'll be."

"Go, get one of ours if you don't mind, Ev. Olga wasn't in our room so not on our team. Let's compare the two. Figure out where they are not the same."

Olga stood there with her forehead scrunched. "Why would they be different though?"

"Exactly my question." Wanda began to study the puzzle again, but she had a hard time recalling what other clues had been on theirs. Think, think. She closed her eyes to try and visualize it, but the image blurred.

A few minutes later Evelyn returned. "Here you go."

Wanda placed the two side by side.

Sure enough, on Olga's the crossword pattern differed and so did the questions.

"This doesn't make any sense." Olga shifted her gaze back and forth between Wanda and Evelyn.

Wanda shoved her lips to one side and thought for a moment. "We split up by rooms. Could it be someone gave us in Room Five a different one on purpose, knowing we would head for the waterfall?"

Evelyn's head bobbed from one sheet to the other. "And the one about trespassing is not on yours either, Olga."

"So?" Olga shrugged. "What could that mean?"

"That Sandie trespassed on the property." Wanda raised one eyebrow.

"Or someone trespassed on Sandie. Meaning they did something wrong to her." Evelyn pressed her fingernail onto the clue to make her point.

"As in the Lord's prayer. Hmm. Possibly." Wanda scanned down both lists of clues. "Olga's doesn't have the doe clue either. The doe . . . what does that have to do with Sandie? I need to think on that some more."

"Both females?" Olga shrugged.

Evelyn snapped her fingers. "Hart. Sandie's last name. A hart is a doe."

The three stared at each other for a minute.

Then Olga shook her head. "Do you two honestly

think someone knew about Sandie's disappearance and set out to get y'all to find her? Since she disappeared on Thursday it would take some fast thinking to appear on a crossword puzzle on Friday morning."

"She has a point, Wanda." Evelyn folded her arms.

"Maybe, but it could be done. They could have chosen us because we three have helped solve crimes before in our town." Wanda sighed. Could it be true?

"In Texas, Wanda. But how would whoever designed the scavenger hunt know that? We didn't exactly put that as our occupation on the applications."

"Well, I sorta did Ev. I put that I was the neighborhood watch chairperson and assisted the police in investigations." Wanda felt her cheeks warm. "And I do have a social media page showing pictures of my awards for solving the Ferguson murders and the accommodation from Tom Jacobs in *The Gazette* about how the watch has helped in bringing criminals to justice."

Olga sucked in a breath. "So, you think . . ."

Wanda rose from the bench. "One way to find out. We need to figure out who designed the word puzzles and ask her. Or him."

"And work out the answers to the other distinct clues not on Olga's to see if they have any relevancy." Evelyn nodded her head as if adding an exclamation point to her sentence.

They heard a gong sound.

"Ten-minute warning to head back for dinner." Evelyn rubbed her stomach. "No wonder I'm getting hungry."

"Dinner?" Wanda slapped her forehead. "Yikes, I am on duty!"

She started to jog toward the kitchen but turned to yell back at her friends. "Tonight, after dinner and the meeting, come to Room Five, Olga. Together, we will figure this out."

Her friends gave her a thumbs up and waved.

Wanda slid into the backdoor of the kitchen and grabbed an apron, hoping Martha wouldn't sentence her to bread and water for running late.

Julie B Cosgrove

CHAPTER 16

Dinner consisted of oven baked chicken breasts, garlic bread, and a veggie medley of sautéed broccoli, cauliflower, mushrooms, and red peppers. Not Wanda's favorite meal of the retreat but the key lime pie for dessert hit the spot.

After she had helped clean up after the meal, Wanda slipped outside to think. She gazed out into the evening. Fireflies hovered over the grass by the pond, blinking in their fairy-like dance. Cicadas droned their songs as the purple and pink horizon faded to navy like a blanket of peacefulness hugging the earth.

Serenity.

Yet somewhere a teenage girl huddled, possibly scared and homesick. Maybe badly injured. How could Wanda not do anything she could to help her? But heading out in the night alone wouldn't be prudent.

Better wait until they gathered together to examine the puzzles. Maybe they'd hold more clues.

She whispered into the growing darkness. "Hang in there, Sandie. We'll find you. I promise."

With a sigh, she headed back inside to join the group.

W.

The evening discussion talked of grace given to us not of our own merit so we should also give others the benefit of the doubt. This initiated a lively discussion on discernment versus judgement and how we can show grace without being duped by people who only want to manipulate or control us.

Wanda, who had a daughter struggling with drug addiction, listened carefully. She had to admit the food for thought gave her more to chew on than dinner had. Her stomach still felt half full. Would they extend her grace to go get a second piece of pie?

At nine in the evening, one of the ladies brought out her guitar and they sang songs, while Martha passed around a huge tin containing buttered popcorn, cheese flavored popcorn, and kettle corn. Each lady was given a plate divided into three sections to serve themselves. Bottles of soft drinks and juice boxes accompanied their snack.

Much better. Wanda chuckled when she noticed Evelyn take two handfuls of the kettle corn. Guess the veggie medley hadn't been her thing either.

After prayers, the ladies filtered to their rooms. Betty Sue, Wanda, and Evelyn sat on the middle bed studying their crossword puzzle and figuring out the next clue. Betty Sue chose to read it out loud in a tone she probably used often in the classroom when reading a story or passage from literature to her students. "But the father said to his servants, 'Bring quickly the best robe, and put it on him, and put a ring on his hand, and shoes on his feet.' Luke 15:22. How we show grace to those who have returned to the fold."

"Well, it's obvious they wanted us to find the shoe, then. I mean four letters off the s in trespass fits s-h-o-e-s." Wanda wrote it in. "Not much help now."

"Did that mean the person who designed it wanted Sandie to come home? That all would be forgiven?" Evelyn cocked one eyebrow.

"It could." Wanda she drew her knees to her chest.

A tap sounded on their door, and Evelyn let Olga in.

"Hi, Olga. "Wanda waved her inside. "Okay, now that we're all here, Betty Sue, what did Fred say."

"And leave out the gushy parts." Evelyn mimed shoving her finger down her throat.

Betty Sue threw a pillow at her. Then she

repositioned herself on the bed and tucked her legs underneath her. "Well, he does know the principal at West Monroe High, and evidently the school is in a spin over Sandie's disappearance. Several parents have organized search parties in and around the lake, but to no avail."

"No one has thought to travel upriver, then. Interesting since it appears this is where some of her belongings were found." Wanda thought for a moment. "Could it be . . ."

"What?" Olga sat on the edge of the bed.

"Just a thought. But what if we were all given these crossword clues to help locate this lost teen. Not just us three. Kinda like sending out five search parties. We need to know who designed the crosswords, and if the other teams had different ones."

Evelyn sat erect. "True. Olga is in four, which is an even number. Maybe the odd numbers, rooms one and three, had our crossword puzzle and room two had one like hers."

"In other words, we are putting together clues in hindsight that were never meant to be there?" Betty Sue's face drooped.

"No, hon." Wanda patted her shoulder. "Just the opposite. If we combine all the clues from all the puzzles, it may lead us to her location."

"Oh!" Betty Sue perked up again "So, what do we

do now?"

"There are three other rooms. Each of you take one and go ask them if we can borrow their crossword puzzles for a few minutes." Wanda pointed to each person. "Olga, take one. Ev, you take two. Betty Sue, go to room three."

"One. Got it." Olga rose to leave, then stopped. "What reason do we give?"

"I, um . . . maybe to decide a runner up?" Wanda shrugged.

"And what prize would they get? We can't do this without Mary Jane's or Martha's input." She leaned against the door jamb.

"Maybe we need to involve them. Afterall, one of them should know who put this all together." Evelyn swung her legs off the edge of the bed and rose.

"I'm not sure." Wanda cocked her head. "Too many cooks you know . . ."

Betty Sue clapped her hands as if to get them all to pay attention. Then she blushed. "Sorry. Force of habit after decades of teaching." She cleared her throat. "I disagree, Wanda. A young girl is missing. We need all the cooks we can gather. I say honesty is always the best policy. Let's tell them in each room what we suspect and ask for their help. Then if something comes of it, we go talk with Mary Jane and Martha."

Wanda gulped. Her almost life-long friend once

again showed wisdom. "She's right. As usual. Go knock on doors while I continue to work out the rest of the answers on these two. Hopefully they will show us a bit of grace."

The three ladies headed out the door on their new mission.

Five minutes later, they gathered again, each with a crossword puzzle in hand. Wanda wrote the room number on each one. Then she laid them side by side. Two and four matched. So did one and three. But none matched theirs in the fifth room.

"Hmm. That answers a lot of questions." Evelyn folded her arms.

"Yes." Wanda glanced up. "Yet poses quite a few more. Let's go find Martha and Mary Jane. I gather they are in the two bedrooms on the first floor."

Wanda gathered the crossword puzzles, putting them in numerical order. Then her phone rang. Mason. Wanda mouthed to her friends who called then put him on speaker.

"Hey, sorry to call so late. Were you asleep?" His voice came through crackly and in hiccups, but she could understand him.

"No." Wanda winked at the others. "I'm wondering why you aren't."

"Ian's being a fuss budget. He may be cutting a tooth. Vickie and I have been taking turns walking him up and down the hall all evening. He's finally crashed, so I decided to give you a call."

Boy, did Wanda remember those days. "Reception is spotty. Can you speak up without waking him up?"

"Let me go out in the yard. One second."

They waited until he came back on. His voice sounded louder but still a bit choppy. "What have you found out, Mason?"

"Bits, here and there. Sandie has a huge following on social media but lately her posts have sounded darker. Went from all is rosy with the world to disgruntled, almost snarky, and definitely slanted. Leaning on radical and anti-American."

"She broke up with her boyfriend last month and started seeing some guy in college. Could that have anything to do with it?"

"Possibly. She mentions several times, 'According to Chad' or 'Chad says.' Whoever he is, he has influenced her greatly."

"Is he on her friends list?"

"That's the odd thing. The answer is no. And I don't see him responding to her posts and tweets either."

Wanda sat back down on the bed. "Strange, right? I mean you'd think someone who has that much input into her opinions would be more visible. No selfies of them together, then?"

"Nope." Mason became silent for a moment.

At first Wanda wondered if the call had dropped. Then she heard him again. "Vickie has a theory. This Chad dude sounds very controlling. Perhaps he wanted to remain in the shadows, and Sandie spouting off about his viewpoints has shone the light on him a bit too much."

Wanda gazed at her friends. From their wide-eyed expressions, she figured their brains went in the same direction as her own. "So, he silenced her?"

"Could be."

Wanda immediately felt a mutual wave of chilliness wrap around the room.

CHAPTER 17

Wanda thanked Mason and ended the call. She shook her head. "I know teenage girls' heads can be turned but . . ."

Olga rose to her feet. "We may not be able to find this Chad guy, but I bet Flex or Brad know something about him."

"Not if he's in college. He'd move in different circles. I think Brad would have given us his name if he did." Wanda rubbed her temple. "He may not even be from around here."

"You mean perhaps he is visiting relatives?" Evelyn shook her head. "It would have to be for quite some time to strike up a friendship. Remember the breakup occurred three weeks ago."

Olga perked up. "I think you mean that he goes to college in Monroe or in Shreveport but might live somewhere else, even out of state, right Wanda?"

"Exactly."

Betty Sue snapped her fingers. "If so, they may have met up at parties or something."

"Okay, if you two want to call Brad again go ahead. But tread lightly." Wanda climbed off the bed. "I am going to knock on Martha's door and ask her who designed these crosswords and why they are different."

Olga waved her phone, but Betty Sue shook her head. "You go on. He knows you."

"Okay." She left the room, probably to head outside to get better reception.

"What if Martha's asleep? You better see if you see a light under her door first." Betty Sue's left eyebrow arched, which usually meant to pay attention to what she said.

Wanda saluted her then winked.

A smile crept across the stern teacher expression Betty Sue tried hard to maintain. She rolled her eyes and huffed. "Very well, Madam Sleuth. I'm coming with you."

Evelyn's head wobbled back and forth between the women. "What do you want me to do?"

Wanda pointed to the sheets on the bed. "I finished ours and most of Olga's. See how many more you can figure out on all of these and then write the answers down. They may mean something."

"On it." Pleased she had an important assignment, Evelyn reached across to the bedside table for her pen.

Wanda gave her a thumbs up and left the room with Betty Sue at her heels.

They tiptoed but of course stepped on three planks that creaked in the process. That brought Martha out of her room at the end of the stairwell to see who snuck downstairs.

Wanda stopped on a dime, which made Betty Sue bump into her backside.

"Ladies? Need a midnight snack?"

The mantle clock had just dinged ten, but Wanda decided not to belabor the point. "Actually, we came to see if you were still awake. Mind if we ask you a question?"

"Not at all. Let's chat in the living room."

She eased the door closed until a barely audible click sounded. Then she motioned for the two ladies to join her.

Once seated on the sofa, Martha held out her hands. "Now, how can I help you two?"

Betty Sue glanced at Wanda.

Wanda took it as a gesture to go first so she did. "We were talking about the clues to the scavenger hunt with Olga Westheimer. Her face became puzzled because her answers differed from ours."

Martha momentarily blanched but then recovered.

"I see. Well, she is in a different room."

"Why were not all the questions and answers alike?" Betty Sue jumped into the conversation with an innocent tone in her voice.

"Oh, Rachel decided she didn't want everyone rushing to the identical locations all at once and stumbling over each other. So, she asked Flex to come up with three versions to spread everyone out over the entire retreat grounds."

"That makes sense." Wanda tried to sound convinced to keep the woman from becoming defensive. "So, you're saying Flex wrote them on his own?"

"Yes. Such a nice young man." Martha clasped her hands and beamed.

"Did Flex make them up while he and the team stayed here?"

"I don't believe so. He drove up to help us haul in the perishable groceries just before everyone arrived on Thursday. I think he handed them to Rachel then along with the lanyards he'd printed off for everyone."

"Well, he did an excellent job. I design word puzzles for our local newspaper. I'd love the chance to talk with him. Perhaps we could publish some of his."

Betty Sue's head jerked in Wanda's direction. Wanda noticed it out of the corner of her eye, but she ignored her friend and continued to focus on Martha's face.

The retreat coordinator smiled. "I read through them, and all the clues appeared equally as hard to solve so I agree. He is quite talented. I'll mention it to Rachel in the morning. Maybe you can chat before the retreat ends."

"I'd appreciate it. Thanks." Wanda scooted forward on the sofa cushion. "Mind if I finish ours? I hate to leave things undone. I can do so in our free time."

Martha's expression eased as if her mind had melted of all doubt. She leaned over and patted Wanda's knee. "Of course. Of course." She stood up and yawned. "Well, ladies, I bid you adieu. Sleep well."

She wrapped her robe around her and shuffled off to her room in her bedroom-slippered feet.

Betty Sue waited until the woman's footfall silenced. "Smooth move."

Wanda sat back and grabbed a throw pillow to hug. "I wonder if Rachel knew the clues might be related to Sandie's disappearance. Or did Flex have an idea where Sandie had disappeared to and with whom, but not wanting to get one of his friends in trouble made up the clues himself so one of us would locate her."

Betty Sue gasped. "You think he wrote them out Thursday just before he came to help his grandmother."

Wanda gave her friend a slow nod. "I don't recall Mason saying exactly when Sandie went missing on

Thursday. If it was in the morning, that would give Flex ample time."

Betty Sue's now wide-awake eyes grew larger. "You think?"

Wanda grinned. She'd hooked her friend's interest at last. "Let's go see if Evelyn has made much progress. I want to finish solving them tonight if all possible."

"We'll need coffee then."

"No, the aroma might wake others up. Grab some chocolate. It has caffeine, right?"

"Okay. I'll go. You keep watch."

Betty Sue snuck off to the kitchen, her body language imitating the stealth of a cat burglar going after the family heirlooms.

Wanda stifled a laugh.

CHAPTER 18

When Wanda entered the bedroom, she found Evelyn deep in concentration. She glanced up and gave Wanda a slight nod.

"I'm almost done. What did you two find out?"

Wanda told her what Martha had revealed. Evelyn leaned back against the headboard with a sigh. "I guess it makes sense. As long as the crossword clues offered the same difficulty in solving and so far, they do. At least to me." She motioned Wanda over.

Wanda sat on the edge of the bed and peered at the crossword puzzle sheets. "Whatcha got?"

Evelyn scooted forward. "I isolated the clues that are the same. For instance, the first answer on ours is trespassing. No one else had it. Nor did they have two or three on ours."

"So . . ."

"But the fifth clue on ours from Acts 11 talks about being saved by grace. It is the first clue for room four's and two's sheet and the third for room one and three. So logically, if what Martha stated is true, we'd all be heading to the life savers hanging by the pond at different intervals."

"I see what you mean. Do you think that's significant?"

"Don't know. It could mean we all were to save Sandie. It's either very important or not at all. One other clue appears on all three examples. 'Give ear, O Lord, to my prayer; listen to my plea for grace' from Psalm 86:6."

"Okay?"

"I figured ear and listen are the likely candidates, and when I tried to fit them in with the other answers, the word ear fit each time. So, unless we find someone's bloody ear on the ground—and I hope we don't . . ." She let out a deep sigh. " . . . I am guessing it is to lead us to the ears of corn they put out for the squirrels on the feeder near the porch."

"Hmm."

A creak of hinges revealed Betty Sue sneaking in with a handful of bite sized chocolate bars. Evelyn made a slurping sound and took one with peanuts. Wanda knew Betty Sue preferred the dark chocolate, so she took a milk chocolate one.

In between bites, they filled Betty Sue in on what they discovered on the crosswords.

"What you are saying, Ev, is that we should concentrate on the dissimilar clues?"

"That's my guess. Do you agree, Wanda?"

"I'm still working out the ears of corn and the squirrels." She chuckled and grabbed a piece of candy that had rice crackles in it, which gave Evelyn the excuse to snatch another one with peanuts. "Perhaps they have nothing to do with anything since they are found on all three."

"Meaning?" Evelyn narrowed her eyes.

"I'm thinking Flex composed the other two then altered ours alone at the last minute. He made three instead of two, one for the odd numbered rooms and one for the even numbered ones, then one for us."

"Why target us?" Bety Sue grabbed the last dark chocolate bar.

"Well, we were the last to register. Maybe he made the others first and then made up ours at the last minute." Evelyn licked her fingers.

Wanda shrugged. "Logical. Which means these could all really mean something or be a huge coincidence."

All three drooped their shoulders. After a few minutes of silence, Wanda spoke again.

"Wait. Martha said he made the lanyards."

"So?" Betty Sue scrunched her nose.

"So, he'd have known we were from Scrub Oak. He may have wondered why we came all this way and out of curiosity did a quick internet search."

"Which would reveal our pertinacity to sleuth. I mean yours, dear." The light in Betty Sue's eyes brightened.

"Exactly." Wanda winked. "And that gave him the idea to alter our puzzle, so we'd help find Sandie. But why?"

Betty Sue glanced around. "Where is Olga? Is she still talking to Brad?"

Prickles ran down Wanda's arm as she glanced at the clock. "For over a half hour? I kinda doubt it."

Evelyn rose. "Let's go find her. I have a weird suspicion something is wrong."

Wanda lifted herself from the bed. "Me too. We better take our phones so we have flashlights and can get in touch with help, if we can get enough bars."

Betty Sue held hers up. "I only have two now. I read once that even if you can't call, sometimes you can text. Let's try it."

She texted her friends and their phones pinged. They returned the text and her phone pinged.

With thumbs up, the three made plans.

Betty Sue reminded them that she had a stronger signal outside when she phoned Fred. "And we were outside when Olga phoned Brad the first time. Maybe she went out there again."

"Good point." Wanda winked. "Betty Sue, you look around inside the cabin, just in case. Check the bathrooms, kitchen, and the screened-in back porch. Evelyn, check around the grounds by the pond and I will check the parking lot. Anyone know what car she drove?"

Evelyn snapped her fingers. "I saw her key chain. It had an Audi medallion."

"Way to go, Ev." Wanda gave her a thumbs up gesture.

Betty Sue wiggled her fingers in goodbye and tiptoed down the hall to the front staircase. Wanda and Evelyn snuck down the back stairs that led outside to the kitchen stoop. Then they went in their separate directions.

Wanda walked flatfooted to avoid her heels crackling the gravel path as she entered the front of the cabin. She headed to the larger parking lot in the clearing. In the new moon's light, she could barely make out the reflecting taillights in the rows of cars. Six lined up on the right next to Martha's van and four lay across the way, including hers. She walked behind each one on the right checking for auto manufacturer symbols on the trunks. No Audis.

A piercing screech jolted her.

She gasped and dropped her phone.

A swoosh brushed overhead. As she ducked with her hands on her head, her eyes caught a shadowed movement. Gazing up, she detected the wingspread of an owl. It swooped upward and settled on a branch on the other side of the parking lot.

Hand to her thudding heart, Wanda took three deep breaths. Then she picked up her phone and examined the screen. Good, no cracks in the glass. She swiped to bring the flashlight app alive again then stared at the feathered creature gazing back at her.

The thing bobbed its head.

She waggled a finger at it and scolded it in a harsh whisper. "Don't ever do that again, bird. Now shoo!"

Voicing another screech, it lifted from the branch and swept down at an angle over one of the cars, then rose toward the moon and flew off.

Wanda's focus followed the barn owl's movement then halted back on the vehicle. The driver's side door appeared to be cracked open, though no light shown inside.

She eased over the gravel as quietly as she could to get a closer view.

No dings warned of the car door being ajar, so the keys must not be in the ignition. The symbol on the trunk showed a series of interlinking circles. An Audi.

As she approached, she saw a shoe dangling out of

the door.

Wanda steadied her trembling hand as she reached for the door handle and gave it a jerk.

Olga's body splayed across the front seats.

"Olga!"

No response.

Wanda called her name louder.

The woman didn't budge. She lay there, still and silent. Her head faced downward onto the upholstery.

In the sparse moonlight, Wanda noticed a dark, wet substance covered part of Olga's hairline and dripped down her temple. A slight odor of iron whiffed from inside the car. Blood.

Wanda's knees wobbled as she grabbed the door jamb to keep her balance.

Julie B Cosgrove

CHAPTER 19

"Please, please, please. Give me bars." Wanda hissed the command to her phone. She called 9-1-1, then texted her friends.

Go wake up Martha. Found Olga in her car. Unconscious. Called 911.

She hesitated to reach across the steering wheel or open the passenger door to feel for a pulse. Part of her didn't want to know the result. The other warned her about disturbing a crime scene, something Todd had scolded her about quite a few times.

Instead, she waited—probably three minutes though it felt like thirty. A shiver zipped through Wanda's skin. She tugged her at T-shirt sleeves. At least she'd had the sense enough to change from her capris into jeans after sunset.

Two women dashed down the lane, one in a robe.

Betty Sue and Martha rushed toward her as Evelyn rounded the building on the other side from the direction of the pond in the back.

All three merged into a group and halted a few feet from the back of the car, as if an invisible line separated them from the scene.

Betty Sue's hand shook as she raised it to her mouth.

Martha breathed an invocation to God. "Is she . . ."

"Not sure. She isn't responding." Wanda felt a stinging in the back of her eyes. She blinked and swallowed.

The faint sounds of a siren echoed through the trees from the direction of the highway.

Martha called Rachel and George. "Go open the gate. We've had an accident here and the EMS are on the way." She clicked off and switched her attention to the three ladies. "Their house is near the entrance. George always locks the gate at dusk unless we tell him otherwise. Of course, I guess the EMS could cut the chain, but . . ." Her voice trailed away.

The three turned their heads to view the unpaved road and listened as the sound grew in volume. A whoop-whoop called out, then the siren started up again. Red lights flashed and bounced through the tree limbs and soon the tires of the emergency vehicle crackled the gravel.

Martha trotted down the lane, waving her hands in the air once she noticed the headlights heading their way.

Almost simultaneously with the vehicle halting, two men jumped out carrying suitcases.

"Here. In the car." Martha motioned to them.

Wanda realized that she, along with Betty Sue and Evelyn, all pointed as well. She swallowed hard and prayed they'd found her new friend in time.

The attendants hurried to the car. One crouched down and opened the cases. Another went to the passenger side and reached in to examine Olga.

Betty Sue's hand grasped Wanda's. She squeezed back.

Then they heard one of the EMT's call out. "Got a pulse."

"Thank, God." Wanda's knees gave way and she slunk to the dirt.

Betty Sue whimpered, and Evelyn sniffled.

Rachel and George ran toward them down the path.

One of the EMT's took pictures as the other huddled in the car over Olga. They muttered to each other and scurried quicker than ants when a cake crumb lands in their path.

Martha and George whispered back and forth. Rachel watched with her hands wrapped around her waist.

Wanda, Betty Sue, and Evelyn huddled together. In her peripheral vison, Wanda noticed several women standing on the front porch. The sirens and lights must have aroused them from their sleep. She motioned to Martha who then twisted around and gazed at the small crowd.

She nodded to Wanda and strolled over to speak with them.

"What do you think happened?" Evelyn whispered the question near Wanda's ear.

"Don't know. But I think someone bashed her on the head. In the moonlight I saw what appeared to be blood matted in her hair." She pointed to her left temple area. "The driver side window is rolled down. I'm guessing she was on the phone when someone reached in . . . wham!"

"What makes you say that?"

A baritone male voice made her jump.

Wanda grabbed her throat and turned to see a uniformed man with his eyebrows forming one line across his forehead.

"Sorry. Didn't mean to startle you. Captain Magnus Roberts. West Monroe Fire Department. And you are . . ."

"Wanda Lee Warner. I am the one who called."

"Seems to me you have a good idea of what happened. I've notified the police. They're on the way."

"Then you expect foul play?"

His lips moved into a tight smile. "Let's wait over here. I'm sure they will want to have a chat, huh?"

Wanda glanced in George's direction as she and the captain walked several cars away. His eyes followed her.

Wait. Did his mouth form a scowl before he looked away again? Why? Wanda filed that tidbit away in her mind to chew on later. Right now, she had other things to occupy her thoughts.

"Is Olga gonna be okay?" Wanda swallowed her emotions down for the third time.

"So, you can positively identify her as Olga Westheimer, right?"

Wanda's mouth opened then closed again.

His expression softened. "Found the car registration in the glove box. She had no ID on her, though."

Wanda ran her hand through her hair. "Um, yes. That's definitely Olga. We are all here on a retreat." She swiveled and motioned toward the women huddled on the porch. "Olga went to use her phone. Reception is spotty in the cabin, so I guess she came out here to her car. She'd been gone a while and we got worried."

"Who?"

"Betty Sue, Evelyn and I." She pointed to Evelyn and Betty Sue now standing near the McDavids and

Martha. "We split up and went in search of her. I . . . found her."

The man laid a hand on her shoulder. "To answer your question, she is still unconscious, but her pulse is stronger. Unless you are her next of kin, that is all I can reveal."

"No, I'm not. You taking her to the hospital then?"

He didn't answer. Instead, his focus redirected to a new vehicle barreling down upon them. The police had arrived.

A humongous, uniformed man, who reminded Wanda of a bouncer in a film noir, emerged from the vehicle. Its driver's side wheels dipped a bit as he did. His partner exited from the other side. The EMT sergeant chatted with them for a few minutes, pointing in the direction of Wanda and her friends who had moved out of the way and were standing on the path by the porch a few feet from Rachel, Martha, and George. The other ladies had disappeared inside.

The two officers meandered over. The larger one's badge read Humphrey, which Wanda figured was his last name, not first.

He raised his chin. "Which one of you called 9-1-1."

"She did." Betty Sue pointed at Wanda.

Thanks, Betty Sue. Wanda suddenly felt like the kid left in front of the neighbor's smashed in window with everyone else's gloves and bats lying at her feet. "Yeah, me." Wanda raised her hand to her shoulder's height then shoved it back down.

"Uh-huh. I am Sergeant Adam Humphrey of the West Monroe police, and this is Officer Gregory Black. You want to explain what's going on?"

Wanda spelled it all out for the police officers including the crossword puzzles and her suspicion they might have something to do with Sandie's disappearance. Evelyn and Betty Sue interceded their comments here and there.

Humphrey kept cocking an eyebrow as if he couldn't decide if what they said made sense or not. Then he'd grunt as he jotted notes in his iPad. The screen's tint exaggerated his facial features in a grueling sort of way. Wanda noticed he never smiled at all.

And, what did those grunts mean? Did he think them dowdy senior citizens bordering on dementia? Another thought whacked her in the heart, then head. Or did he think they made up the whole thing?

Could he really suspect one of them of doing this to Olga? Didn't they always suspect the first people on the scene? As if she'd ever whack someone on the head. Or Evelyn. Definitely not Betty Sue. But he didn't know them from . . . well, not Adam. That was *his* name. Maybe from Eve either. Oh, dear, now her thoughts babbled. She sucked in a breath to calm her nerves.

She felt like telling him about the crimes she'd help solve, along with her two friends, over the past few years. *Want my credentials as Scrub Oak's neighborhood watch chairperson and organizer, son? Want to see the accommodations on my social media page? How about I phone my town's chief of police, or the mayor for that matter.*

Instead, she zipped her lip. Show grace. Show grace... *it's late at night and the man probably had been woken from a sound sleep.*

He finished tapping in his notes then half-thanked, half-grunted to the three of them.

Wanda tried to keep her temper at bay, but oh, how she wished Todd could be here.

Then it hit her, as sometimes ideas do. Why couldn't he? She needed his support and advice. Maybe intervention. More than an attorney.

And perhaps he could help her connect the dots—unofficially of course. Like a consultant.

As Officer Humphrey walked over to speak with George, Wanda slipped her phone from her pocket and dusted it off. Its clock flashed 11:30. Todd would be on duty.

"What are you doing?" Betty Sue leaned in and

hissed in her ear.

"I'm calling Todd."

"Why?"

Wanda blinked to keep the tears from forming. Her voice shook a bit as she responded. "I need him here."

Betty Sue patted her arm. "Of course, you do. I wouldn't mind his presence either."

Wanda stepped off the path, then slammed into the wide chest of the other policeman. She sucked in a breath, along with the scent of his musky aftershave. It almost overwhelmed her.

His utility belt let off a leathery squeak as Officer Black laid his hand on the holster.

"Ma'am. We need you to stay put."

"I, um. I want to make a phone call to my nephew. He's, well, kinda like my guardian." *We are allowed one phone call, right?* Wanda shook that thought away before it hit her tongue. No one had arrested her . . . yet. She'd already been falsely accused and hauled in once this year in Scrub Oak. She didn't relish the idea of a repeat.

She put on her sweetest little old lady expression. "Lousy reception inside the cabin. I won't go far, Officer Black. Promise."

The man didn't appear affected by her act. Maybe she was losing her touch. "If you like, I will stand behind your cruiser."

George, or someone else, had turned on the flood lights and one of them shone directly onto the squad car.

Black nodded.

"Thanks. I won't be long. Promise."

Had she just said the word promise twice? She cringed a bit as she slithered away, swiping her contacts app. She chose her nephew's cell phone number and hit the phone icon.

As she did, the EMS van's siren revved up as it carried off Olga.

Todd answered on the second ring. "Aunt Wanda? Is that a siren? I thought you were on that retreat."

"I am." At the sound of his voice, the dam broke and all the emotion she'd pushed down for the past half hour or so spilled out into tears. "Oh, dear boy. I need you."

CHAPTER 20

After Wanda explained the situation, Todd remained silent for a minute. She wondered if he had become angry with her for calling him. Or frustrated because she had once again stumbled into a crime.

She opened her mouth to explain it wasn't her fault. She didn't purposely go looking for bloody shoes and socks or go on a retreat because a teenage girl had gone missing nearby. And to tell Todd how she hated to be in the midst of an investigation again. Well, not exactly true. Sleuthing pumped her blood a bit harder. It made her feel worthwhile, needed, and—dare she say it? Sharp-minded still.

Then she heard his sigh through the phone.

"Aunt Wanda. I need to finish my shift. I will drive straight there when I get off at six so you will see me about eleven tomorrow morning."

She let out the breath she didn't realize she'd been holding. "Thank you, Todd. I'd feel ever so much better if you were here. I think Ev and Betty Sue would as well."

"I have no jurisdiction, you realize."

"Yes, I do. But you do have expertise in police protocols and perhaps you can—"

"—be your sleuth partner? Absolutely not. Drop the ball, Aunt Wanda. It's not yours to pass."

"But a young girl is missing, and we are ninety-nine percent sure we found her shoe and socks. Doesn't that give me some responsibility?"

"Yes. To report it. Which you have. You don't need to do anything more at this point. I don't want to drive over there simply to post bail because you got in the way of their investigation."

She figured he'd say that. If she rolled her eyes would Todd be able to detect the gesture over the phone? However, she knew her compliance would be the lure to draw him to Louisiana. And she wanted him here to guide her and her friends. So, she backed down. "I understand. Okay, I promise to behave until you can get here."

That made him chuckle, then his voice took on a serious tone again. "Now, listen to me, Aunt Wanda. Do *not* volunteer any more information than you already have until I arrive, got it?"

She switched the phone to her other ear. "What if they want to interrogate me?"

"Tell them you will answer all their questions as soon as your advocate comes and give them my ETA, so they know you are not stalling but being compliant. It's your right to have someone present with you."

"Even if I'm not in Texas?"

"Yes, ma'am. It's federal law except in some misdemeanor cases. This isn't one of those."

She felt her neck and shoulder muscles ease. "Todd?"

"Yeah?"

"Thank you doesn't begin to cover this. Drive safely, okay?"

She could almost hear his grin through the phone. "See ya soon. Love ya."

"Love you back." She sent up a prayer of thanksgiving for having Todd for a nephew and sauntered back to her friends, avoiding the scrutinous eyes of the patrolman stationed on the steps.

Then she stopped. No, she should act better than this. Why be defensive? It might send the wrong vibes. *Show grace*, a voice whispered into her soul.

She raised her gaze to meet his eyes. "Officer? Thank you for allowing me to make that phone call. I greatly appreciate your consideration. It relived me a great deal to talk to my nephew after that horrific experience of finding Mrs. Westheimer all bloody and slumped over in her car."

The man's cheeks flushed as he sputtered, "You're welcome, ma'am." Then he dashed his gaze back to the parking lot where his colleague wound crime tape around the area.

Wanda's spirits lifted after showing him a smidgen of grace. Maybe she had learned something this weekend after all.

W₄

By the expression on their faces, Evelyn and Betty Sue seemed relieved that Todd would be heading their way. They told Wanda they'd overheard one of the EMTs say Olga had regained consciousness as they loaded her into the ambulance. Even though she appeared lucid, they told George and Rachel they would be transporting her to the hospital for observation.

"That's great news." It felt as if fifty pounds of worry slid off her chest, though it irked her that George – also not a next of kin – got the news. She guessed maybe they all lived nearby and knew each other. "I don't see me getting much shut eye, though. Still too tightly wound."

"Me, too." Betty Sue blew out a long breath.

Evelyn agreed. "My heart is still playing a rap

tune."

"Think we'd be allowed to make a pot of coffee?"

"I believe Martha already thought of that. Seems insomnia is epidemic tonight." Betty Sue motioned to the windows that lined one wall of the living room, Through the blinds, Wanda detected several of the other attendees had gathered in huddles. Some held styrofoam cups. A large silver urn sat on the side table.

"Let's go." She went to the front door then stopped. "Excuse me, sir?" She twisted back and addressed the patrolman near the steps again. "Okay if we get a cup of coffee?"

He shrugged.

"Do you want one, too, sir?"

His stone face softened a tad. "Thank you. Black."

"Coming right up." Wanda grinned.

Evelyn followed closely behind. "New friend?"

"Hopefully. Prefer that to an enemy. These Louisiana cops are huge!"

Betty Sue giggled. "When will Todd get here?"

"Tomorrow morning. About eleven. Until then, he said for us not to offer any more information but to tell the police we will gladly speak with them once he shows up as our advocate."

Evelyn handed out the cups and poured herself one. "You're thinking they suspect one of us, right?"

"Well, Ev, as your shows often say, everyone is

treated as such until proven otherwise. And we were the last people known to be with her."

"Yeah. Right." She sighed and moved out of the way to add sugar to her brew. "Except we weren't. Whoever conked her was. If only we could prove it."

The worry lines on Betty Sue's forehead deepened.

Wanda touched her arm. "It's going to be fine."

Now to convince herself of that.

CHAPTER 21

Wanda had barely raised her cup to her lips when Martha clapped to get everyone's attention.

"Great news. Rachel McDavid called from the hospital. Olga is awake and talking. She has a slight concussion, so they are keeping her overnight for observation just in case. Otherwise, vital signs are good."

Murmurs of gratitude floated through the room. Someone suggested they pray and thank the Lord. So, they all bowed their heads. As they finished, footsteps entered the room. Wanda raised her eyes to view the policeman she had met before. Martha spoke again. "Officer Mulligan would like to say a few words. Most of you already know him, of course."

Something about him tickled the corners of her mind, a vague notion that had not caught her attention the first time they met.

The man stepped forward with his hands tucked into his utility belt, which held all sorts of police equipment. His stride reminded Wanda of a bulldog. His stature and demeanor demanded attention. She doubted very many criminals dared to challenge his authority. Something about him tickled the corners of her mind. She squinted to draw it closer to the surface as she listened to his spiel.

"Ladies, it is late. I realize that. So, I will be sending a team to interview each of you to get some idea of Olga's movements and activities here. Let's meet up here in the morning after breakfast about 10:00, okay?"

Betty Sue turned to Wanda and whispered. "Prayer answered! Surely they will interview those she rode with first."

Wanda agreed. Her attention returned to his voice.

"But for now, until we learn more, I am strongly encouraging each of you to limit your wanderings to inside this facility, and to be in pairs as much as possible."

"What?" A female voice squawked. "Do you think whoever hurt her is lurking around here?"

Several ladies gasped.

A few grabbed the hand of someone next to them.

Evelyn stepped forward. "You think the perp is still out there. That we might be in danger?"

Wanda took a deep breath. Under her breath she whispered for Evelyn to shush up and not draw unnecessary attention to themselves.

Betty Sue rolled her eyes. "Too late. She said the word 'perp'."

The officer shifted his weight. "Ma'am, this isn't CSI. Whatever you watch on TV is rarely reality. But until we speak with Mrs. Westheimer and get her statement, we think it wise for the rest of the group to be cautious."

His raised eyebrow, along with the semi bulldog stance made Evelyn zip her lips. She glanced at the floor and nodded like a student being reprimanded for talking in class.

Satisfied, he turned back to scan the other ladies. "We will be able to address your questions more tomorrow. For now, try to get a good night's sleep and please, stay away from the parking lot. It is a crime scene and must be preserved. Thank you."

He tipped his hat as he flashed them a narrow smile and left the room. Maybe the man simply felt uncomfortable in a room filled with ladies in their pjs and robes. Wanda could understand that.

Martha cleared her throat. "Well, I for one have had two cups of coffee so I am wide awake now."

Nervous giggles filtered through the attendees.

"I had planned chocolate pecan pie bars for

tomorrow's desert. But if anyone would like to join me in the kitchen to make some now, I'd welcome the help. They should be piping hot and gooey in about twenty minutes or so."

Several ladies raised their hands, Betty Sue included, which made Wanda do a doubletake. Miss Health Nut, never-let-sugar-touch-my-tonsils volunteered to make a decadent desert? She had to be stressed out.

The rest of the women played cards, chatted, or read their Bibles and waited as the delicious aroma of butter, chocolate, and vanilla drifted from the kitchen.

Mary Jane manned her book table with pursed lips under dancing eyes trying not to appear too pleased that she'd been granted more time for the attendees to browse her works.

Evelyn drifted away and took an unusual interest in the guest book pages. She probably wanted to sink into the woodwork after being reprimanded.

Wanda smothered a snicker with her hand and headed back to their room to ponder the puzzles. Then she halted halfway up the stairs. Wait. No. Evelyn would not have been daunted for long. She had begun investigating again.

Now that brain-tickle she experienced when the policeman talked floated to the forefront of her mind. Wanda dashed back down the stairs just as Evelyn's eyes met hers.

Evelyn's mouth moved into a smug grin as she pointed to the guest book.

Wanda felt a frostiness zip through her veins. "Mulligan, right?"

Her friend winked. "I had to see the name again to make sure. But yes. Aiden Mulligan stayed here a few weeks ago and, from what we've been told, he is Sandie's ex-flame. We need to pull up the wrestling team's web page to see if he and our investigating officer resemble each other."

"Let's go."

Evelyn grabbed her sleeve. "After we get our pecan bars."

Right. They had all night to work this out. Afterall, life had set-in-stone priorities and a gooey chocolate desert warm from the oven topped the list.

CHOCOLATE PECAN PIE BARS

Ingredients:

- 2 cups flour
- ½ teaspoon sea salt
- ½ cup of powdered sugar

- 1 cup butter – I use Kerrygold Irish butter. It is extra creamy and favorable.
- 1 14 ounce can of sweet, condensed milk – Do NOT use evaporated milk.
- 1 egg, beaten
- 1 teaspoon vanilla extract – Mexican vanilla if you can find it.
- 1 cup finely chopped pecan halves
- 12 package of semi-chocolate baking chips
- 1 package of Heath toffee brickle bits – If you can't find that, then finely smash 3-4 peanut brittle candies.

Directions:

1. Preheat the oven to 350° F, or lower to 325° F if you have a glass or Pyrex dish.
2. In a medium mixing bowl, blend together the dry ingredients then fold in the butter with a pastry cutter or fork until coarsely crumbled. Press that in the bottom of a greased 9x12 pan. Bake for 15 minutes.
3. In the meantime, beat the condensed milk and egg together, then blend together the rest of the ingredients.
4. Remove the pan from the oven and let it cool five minutes or so. Then evenly spread the nut and candy mixture over the top with a spatula.

5. Return the pan to the oven and bake for another 25 minutes until golden brown.

6. Let it cool completely and then cut it lengthwise into four strips. Cut each of those into rectangular bars about as long as your little finger.

7. Store it in a tightly lidded container in the fridge.

8. Makes about 36 bars.

Julie B Cosgrove

CHAPTER 22

Thank the Lord for a sudden strong Wi-Fi signal.

Wanda swiveled her laptop and nodded. "Okay. We've established that Aiden is definitely related to Officer Mulligan. Possibly a dad or uncle. But where does that lead us?"

"Could be coincidence. I mean they all live close to here, right?" Betty Sue sat cross-legged on the bed.

"She's right." Evelyn wiped some residual chocolate from the corner of her mouth. "We still do not know if any of this has anything to do with Sandie's disappearance. Olga could have been attacked by a burglar."

Wanda shook her head. "She had nothing on her. Her phone still lay on the floorboard."

"Maybe he thought she called 9-1-1?" Evelyn shrugged.

"Okay, let's put that aside for now until we can perhaps speak with her." Wanda eyed them both.

Her friends nodded in agreement.

"Let's refocus on the crossword puzzle clues to see if they have anything to do with finding Sandie." Wanda grabbed the papers and spread them out across the bed.

W.

Two hours later, the sugar rush from the pecan bars had faded and the caffeine effects had waned. Wanda yawned, which set off tacit responses from Evelyn and Betty Sue that they, too, wanted to call it a night. Downstairs, the faint chime of the mantle clock struck one.

With a stretch of her hands over her head, Wanda conceded. "It appears that doe, trespass, apple, and pour are the only clues on our puzzle that didn't appear on any of the others. My guess is Flex saw Sandie's shoe, recognized it, and then set out to tell us she, a Hart, trespassed where the brook begins to pour."

"Makes sense to me." Evelyn rubbed her eyes. "Now can we get some sleep?"

Betty Sue's eyelids were half closed as well.

"Yep. Sorry. I forgot you have breakfast duty tomorrow morning, Ev."

"I'll sleep fast." She waddled to her bed and

plopped her head onto her pillow with her back to them.

Wanda came over to her and gently jostled her shoulder. "Wake me up when you do. I want to go with you and speak with Rachel about interviewing Flex."

"Huh?" Evelyn twisted back to view Wanda's face.

"About writing puzzles for *The Gazette*, and then asking him about the clues."

"But we've already solved them." Betty Sue crawled under her covers as she spoke.

"Yes, but why go to all this elaborate ruse? Why not simply tell his grandmother he thought he'd found Sandie's shoe?"

Betty Sue sat back against the headboard. "Because he didn't want to be the one who found it?"

"Bingo." Wanda pointed at her. "That's why I want to chat with him."

"Tomorrow . . ." Evelyn yawned the word.

"Yes, tomorrow." Wanda went to her bed and reached to turn off the lamp.

She heard Evelyn's soft snores as she did. *Sleep fast is right.*

Her brain, however, wouldn't cooperate. She lay awake staring at the ceiling, watching the shadow of the leaves sway in the moonlight.

Any good whodunnit answered the questions who, when, where, and why.

Who? She still didn't have a clue as to who Sandie

disappeared with—if anyone.

Or to where.

When had to be before two in the afternoon, otherwise Flex wouldn't have had enough time to find out about it and design the crossword clues. Perhaps Mason could look at the press releases or police reports to determine when she was first reported missing.

And why?

God only knew, and He was not revealing anything to her . . . yet.

W,

Wanda must have fallen asleep because it took a moment for her brain register Evelyn shaking her shoulder.

"Pssst. Wake up."

Her eyes flashed open as her heart pounded in her throat. "What?"

"Sshh. Betty Sue is still asleep. Time to get up."

Wanda's grey cells began to spark. Right. Talk with Rachel. "Gotcha." She unwound herself from the sheets. Ten minutes later the two headed to the kitchen.

"Well, I'll be." Wanda stopped Evelyn and pointed with her head.

A blurry-eyed Flex helped his grandmother carry in sacks.

"God does have His ways." Evelyn winked and reached for an apron.

Wanda held back and waited at the van until Flex appeared again. "Hi, you must be Flex, right?"

The young man halted and stared at her. His eyes darted back to the kitchen door as if he tried to decide to run to his grandmother like a boy or stand his ground like a man. Teenage emotions. So complex.

Wanda put on her sweetest little old lady smile. "Martha told me that you are the clever one who designed the crossword puzzles, yes?"

That relaxed his shoulders a bit. His mouth curved into a smile. "Yes'm."

Wanda moved closer. She told him about her position at the Oakmont County's newspaper. "I wondered if perhaps we might feature one of yours. We have permission to reprint one that is nationally syndicated, but perhaps you could do one that had more of a, well, local spin. We could work together on that. Our news is online so you could read up on a few recent events or ones coming up . . ."

She could see a spark of interest in his eyes.

"Of course, we'd do an article acknowledging you as well. How long have you been designing crossword puzzles, Flex?"

He shuffled his feet as a blush colored his cheeks. "Since junior high. Not too many people know about it though. Just a few close friends, and my parents and grandparents. Being a jock and a nerd don't mix, ya know?"

"Well, it's high time people knew. You are quite talented."

He raised his eyes as the blush deepened. "Really?"

Bait taken, reel him in. "I think so and word games are my thing. We'd pay you of course. I'd have to run it by the editor in chief to determine how much, though. Maybe $50 per puzzle? We publish twice a week."

Now his eyes locked solely onto hers. Evidently $400 a month still meant something to a seventeen-year-old guy. But her conscience reined her in. "That is not a promise now, you understand. I don't have the authority to offer it to you. But I can definitely go to bat for you."

He nodded as his Adam's apple bobbed.

"Let me make a quick phone call. Could we meet up by the pond after breakfast? Say about 9:30?"

"Yes'm. Sure."

She reached to shake his hand and grinned through the pain that shot into her arm. Man, he must be an excellent wrestler with that grip. It reminded her of the time she caught her hand in the automatic car window of her brand-new Toyota back in 1987.

A movement caught her glance. Rachel stood at the doorway, her hand on her hips. "Flex?"

"Hey, Grans. Guess what? Mrs. Warner might hire

me to design crosswords for their local paper. Isn't that cool?"

Rachel gave him a semi-smile then narrowed her gaze at Wanda. Wanda immediately felt her antagonism. What was up with that? She decided to lather on the honey again. If it worked with the grandson it might work with the grandmother.

"I told him I'd talk to my editor-in-chief about it. Flex really has a talent, you know. A rarity these days. Most kids are into computer programming and such."

Rachel's expression softened. "Yes, well Flex is an exceptional young man. And I need him to come bring in the rest of the groceries or breakfast will be late." She gave him a wink and turned to go back into the kitchen.

He rolled his eyes. "Better go now."

Wanda decided to save him any further embarrassment. "See ya later, okay?"

He bobbed his head rapidly then bent to get the next sack along with two jugs of orange juice.

Wanda rounded the building to the path near the parking lot. The yellow crime tape flapped in the early morning breeze, sending renewed chills down her spine. She stepped back and sat down on the front porch stoop. Through the open windows, probably to let the morning coolness inside, she could hear a few voices as ladies came down to grab some coffee. The whiff of bacon cooking made her stomach growl.

Her phone's home page glowed "7:45 AM." Mason should be awake by now. She took the chance and pressed his icon in her contacts.

He answered with a question in his tone. Wanda told him about Flex and could tell by his response he showed interest.

"$50 is a bit steep. How about $40 for a puzzle with 20 clues to start? He can design four of them for us to run on Fridays. After we've judged the popularity for a month we can discuss a contract."

"I think that's fair."

"I would 1099 him though if he contracts with us, so make sure he understands what that involves."

"Will do. One more thing, Mason. Do you have any idea when the report on Sandie Hart's disappearance came out on Thursday?"

"Why?"

"Just trying to establish a timeline."

"Wanda Warner, what have you got your nose into now? I think Todd is a bit peeved at me for feeding you information about her anyway."

"Only because he is worried. The police may think me to be a suspect. He is on his way here by the way. To be my advocate."

"I see."

Did he? "If she disappeared while we were enroute that day, then . . ."

"Ah. You have an ironclad alibi. Hold on."

She waited. A squirrel chastised her for daring to talk underneath his tree. She stuck her tongue out at it, and it scampered away.

"First report I can glean is stamped 1:45 p.m. States she had been missing for at least two hours."

Wanda couldn't help but smile. "Thanks, Mason. At that time, we were eating BBQ at a truck stop in Longview. I have a time stamped receipt."

"Ah, ha."

"I will talk with Flex and then text you his cell phone number along with shots of two of the puzzles he designed for us ladies on the retreat."

The bell dinged meaning breakfast had been placed out on the buffet line. She hung up and dashed inside. As Evelyn brought out a platter of bacon strips, Wanda gave her a thumbs up signal.

Evelyn grinned and set the food down. But before she could speak, the drone of women's voices lining up for food filled the cabin. They'd have to chat later, hopefully before the police returned.

Julie B Cosgrove

After breakfast, Wanda filled her friends in about Flex. Betty Sue pursed her lips.

"What?" Wanda shrugged.

"I am not pleased with your motives." Her teacher tone came through. "You wouldn't be offering this boy a position on *The Gazette* if you didn't want to pump him for information. That's, well, almost lying."

Wanda felt the arrow of conviction stab her heart. "You're right. But we are not sure of his innocence in this whole affair either. It works both ways."

Betty Sue harrumphed and folded her arms over her chest. "You honestly expect him to decline this offer because he is somehow connected with Sandie's disappearance?" She lowered her tone to mimic a teenage boy. "Um, Ma'am, I wish I could accept but you see I have been engaging in criminal activities and if my grandpa were to find out, he'd hang me up to dry."

Evelyn laughed.

Wanda made a shushing sound and pumped her hand for them to lower their volume in case anyone was outside their room. "Very well. But if he does have evidence and comes forward, then I will consider he passed the test and would be a reliable employee."

Betsy Sue rose from the bed. "You have an answer to everything. As long as you get results you don't care who gets hurt in the process." She waggled her finger. "Ask yourself this. Who are you doing this for? Sandie Hart's sake or your own?"

As she stomped away Wanda felt her heart tear. Betty Sue had a point.

Evelyn kept quiet. Bless her.

Wanda shoved her suitcase aside. "Do you agree with Betty Sue?"

Evelyn glanced at her then began making her bed.

Wanda waited, her stomach clenching harder with each passing second.

"Well, she does have a point, but I think she came down on you awfully hard." Evelyn glanced back at her. "I think you have a superwoman complex. You want to save the world. As if it is some divinely appointed task."

Wanda sighed. "Hey, I didn't want to find a bloody sock inside a shoe. These crimes find me. It's not as if I go in search for them."

Evelyn stared into her eyes for a moment. Then she sighed. "You're right. But the average person would simply turn the shoe in to the police and wash their hands of it. Why do you believe it is up to you to do more than that?"

Wanda rested her chin on her hand. "I don't know. I have a problem, don't I?"

Evelyn did a rare thing—for her. She came over and laid her hand on Wanda' shoulder. "You have a big heart and an overly exaggerated sense of duty. You hate anyone being wronged and feel the need to help make things right. You are a do-er."

"W . . . what?" Wanda raised her head and swiveled to face Evelyn.

"You feel you need to do something. You are not one to sit on the sidelines and cheer. You have an innate desire to be in the game."

"And deliver the game-winning play?"

"Well . . . maybe because you know you can. But you don't take the glory. You have turned the limelight onto Todd a lot, you know." Evelyn picked up her pillow and pointed it at Wanda. "That says something in your favor."

Wanda sat back and stared at the watercolor hanging on the wall in front of her. She had never noticed it. The scene showed a bubbling brook in the sheltered woodland cascading down a small hillside.

The serenity of the drawing drew her into the picture. Sunlight played with the leaves and speckled the ground, but some of the golden rays streamed in through a tiny clearing onto a doe bending to take a drink in the far upper corner above the waterfall.

A cold splash hit Wanda's brain. Could it be this was what they were to find all along? In their room, room five? She recalled Betty Sue, or was it Evelyn, mentioning maybe there hung a deer painting in the cabin. Had one of them noticed it but not recalled where? Why had they not searched for it first?

She rose and went over to the framed artwork. Her hand slid behind the frame. Sure enough. Her fingers felt a piece of paper. She gently peeled the tape away and slipped the folded note from its hiding place.

"Whatcha got?"

Wanda jolted, then caught her breath. Evelyn stood behind her. She indicated with her glance for Evelyn to notice the painting.

Evelyn stared for a moment, then her eyes widened as she examined the scene. "It has some of the crossword clues in it."

Then Wanda held up the paper. "This was taped behind it. Kinda cliché, but . . ."

"Open it!"

A smile emerged on Wanda's lips. She quietly unfolded the note.

The computer-typed words read, *Look in the cave.*

Wanda scrunched her eyebrows together. "What cave? Does Louisiana have caves?"

Evelyn lifted one shoulder to her ear. "Ask Flex."

Wanda turned to her as she refolded the note and slid it into her pocket. "I plan to do exactly that. Almost time for me to meet with him. I better brush my teeth."

"The morning session starts at nine. How are you going to slip out?'

"I'll figure that out later. See ya." She grabbed her toiletries bag and dashed to the communal bathroom.

At nine sharp the women gathered in the living room. Wanda sat off to the side near the entrance to the screened in porch. She hoped everyone's attention would be riveted onto Mary Jane's talk in a while and she could sneak out unnoticed. Betty Sue and Evelyn sat on the couch instead. Evelyn gave her a wink.

They started with a brief prayer service then Mary Jane began her lecture. The mantle clock's minute hand had struck the quarter hour tune when the sound of gravel popping caught everyone's attention.

Wanda glanced at her friends. Too soon for Todd and too many tires making the noises.

Martha rose and went to the window. She pulled back the curtain. Her shoulders drooped. She twisted to view the women.

"Ladies. It appears the police have arrived earlier

than we expected. Our morning session is suspended, I guess. Sorry, Mary Jane."

She shrugged and capped her marker.

"It is important we all cooperate. Any information we can give them may lead them to whoever hurt poor Olga, right ladies?"

The decibel of chatter rose as women shuffled to close their Bibles and gather their things.

Wanda figured they had shown up early to first go over the crime scene in the daylight. She edged through the crowd toward the back porch to meet Flex when a hand grabbed her arm.

Martha yanked her back around. "Wanda, you seem to have leadership skills. Will you help me organize the women in an orderly fashion and perhaps think of a way to entertain them as each is interviewed by the police? Mary Jane doesn't want to continue until they are gone. It would be too disruptive."

"Um, well . . ." Wanda stuttered.

The expression reflected in Martha's eyes told her saying no would not be an option. Why single out Wanda for the task? What did the woman know? Had she learned about her meeting with Flex?

Like a mouse staring at a cat crouched near its hole in the baseboard, Wanda felt trapped.

CHAPTER 24

Wanda's skill involved word games and cooking for friends. What could she possible devise to keep fifteen or so women occupied? She sat back down to think.

How did she use to entertain Todd and his friends when they descended on her house? Ah . . . *Charades*.

Wanda asked the ladies to sit together by rooms and then handed each team a note pad.

"This will be mimed, like *Charades*. Each team will act out a scene in the Bible. The other teams will write down what they think it is. Each correct answer gets a point on the white board." She made five columns and numbered them. She noticed Rachel wiping down the coffee bar. "Rachel, will you keep score for us?"

The woman glanced around. How could she say no?

Martha clasped her hands together in approval. Mary Jane gave Wanda huge grin and joined Team Four as Olga's replacement. Martha joined Betty Sue and Evelyn.

About that time, Sergeant Humphrey tapped on the door as he opened it and stepped inside.

Office Black entered behind him, and a female officer followed up the rear. The women hushed and silently followed the three into the room with their eyes.

"Ladies. Good morning. I see a few familiar faces, but I must treat all of you equally so do not be offended if we don't chat." Sergeant Humphrey scanned the women again, and his eyes landed on Wanda's face for a few seconds as she stood off to the side by the whiteboard.

She sucked in a breath and tried not to react.

He blinked and returned his attention to the five groups seated in front of him. "We will be interviewing each of you individually. This is simply to gather information which may help us discover who injured Mrs. Westheimer, so I know each of you are more than willing to help anyway you can."

The ladies nodded, murmured they were, or gave him a small smile. His jawline softened. "Anything you can tell us that you know or have observed would be helpful no matter how insignificant you believe it to be."

He took a breath then continued. "We will ask for

fingerprints as a process of this elimination, but don't worry. No one is in trouble, all right? And no more black fingers. It is all digitally recorded now."

He cracked a smile as several women let out sighs. He turned to Martha. "Can you get me a list of all the participants and then bring them to us one at a time in the order on the list?"

"Yes, sir." She grabbed her clipboard from the table and flipped through it. Then she handed over what Wanda assumed would be the registration print out.

He glanced over the two pages and nodded. "Addresses and phone numbers, too. Very good. Thank you."

Martha's back straightened and a glow appeared on her face. "Perhaps the card game table on the back porch would work well as your station?"

He agreed then addressed the retreat participants once again. "Ladies, Martha will call each of you in order. Please stay in the living area if at all possible. This will save us time. If you must go outside or to the ladies' room, ask permission from Officer Black." He glanced to his left and the man standing next to him responded with a head bob. Wanda recognized him as the one who'd stood guard on the porch last night.

"Officer Stanford and I will be out that door on the back porch waiting for you." The policewoman behind him on his right took a step forward and silently gestured a greeting to the women.

The two started to follow Martha then Humphrey stopped and returned to stand in front of the whiteboard. "Oh, also I must request that you do not discuss your interviews among each other. All right, ladies? That is very, very important."

Every female's head nodded, Wanda's included.

He flashed them all a tight smile and proceeded to the porch, again glancing in Wanda's direction before exiting. She wondered why. Had Olga talked already and described her? More likely Mulligan had briefed him. She had a sneaky suspicion her interview would last the longest.

Wanda took a deep breath. The clock read nine-fifty-five. Flex had probably skedaddled by now. Not that she'd blame him. The good news is she knew Todd would arrive about eleven. And being the game leader, it almost ensured her to be the last to be interviewed. Finding Flex would have to wait.

She assumed her name, along with Betty Sue and Evelyn's, would be the at the end anyway since they had been the last to register. She sent up a prayer that God's timing would be in sync with hers. She really wanted her nephew present for each of their interroga . . . er interviews.

But until then, she had an assignment to perform. She turned to the other women and asked if they were ready to begin the game.

Most of their faces showed enthusiasm and perhaps relief to be kept busy instead of sitting around tapping their toes. Like her, she figured none of them relished the idea of being asked questions by the police, even if several of the ladies probably knew one if not all three of the officers. Maybe even barbequed with them in backyards or church grounds. Something about their uniforms generated a respectful fear. Whose stomach didn't clinch a tad when she saw a patrol car following her vehicle?

Just as Team One began their pantomime, Martha appeared at the door and called the first name. A woman from the third team sighed and rose to follow her.

And so it began . . .

W.

Wanda did her best to keep her attention on monitoring the game. She had given up on straining one ear to catch any of the conversations between the participants and the police as she stealthily stood off to one side of the whiteboard.

Several times Martha winked at her as she called the next name, which Wanda assumed was the woman's way of expressing gratitude. Each interviewed woman returned to her team tight-lipped but with very little, if any, stress covering her face. In fact, most appeared a great deal more relaxed coming out than they had going into the interview area.

The mantle clock chimed ten-thirty. Eight more left to interview, including her, Betty Sue, and Evelyn. Cutting it close.

In the middle of team two's second pantomime, the porch door creaked open, and Humphrey and Stanford entered, then turned into the dining room. Out of the corner of her eye Wanda saw them fill styrofoam cups with coffee and chat a moment.

Taking a break. Good. She muffled a grin by coughing into her fist then grabbing her cup of water. Betty Sue's eyes moved to the clock, then back to her and winked. Evelyn glanced at them both and let out a small sigh through her cheeks. They all were on the same wavelength. Come on, Todd.

Team One guessed the biblical character. Cheers and high fives went up. They were now one point ahead. As the jubilation died down Wanda heard the pop of gravel. A car.

She eyed her friends again as a vehicle's door closed. Then another one shut. Who had Todd brought with him?

The front door opened, and squeals of delight rang out through the room. Wanda turned to see Olga standing there with Rachel. Strips of adhesive angled across her temple near her hairline like a small railroad track. Her complexion had definitely paled but her eyes seemed bright.

Her roommates jumped up to greet her, all chattering at once. Other ladies smiled and commented among each other as a tone of joy and relief filled the room.

Olga's focus deviated from her well-wishers long enough to lock briefly with Evelyn's. Wanda noticed Evelyn mouth a question asking Olga if she was okay. Olga nodded, then grimaced a bit. Her head must still hurt like the Dickens.

As Olga moved through the crowd to sit down with one of her friends, Wanda felt the need to acknowledge her, but as soon as she opened her mouth, Mary Jane stood and took the stage. "Welcome back, dear Olga. We have all been praying for you."

And are dying to drill you for details. At least two of us are. Wanda glanced at Evelyn, and from the expression on her tight lips, Wanda figured her friend's mind wandered in the same direction. Betty Sue just stood there with her hands clasped and a shimmer in her eyes.

That prickled Wanda's conscience. Was it wrong of her to be more concerned about speaking with Olga than finishing the game she had been put in charge of conducting? She convinced herself everyone had lost interest in the charades anyway and edged through the throng of women to catch Olga's eye.

CHAPTER 25

The commotion brought the two police officers into their midst. Sergeant Humphrey stepped forward and asked Olga how she fared. She told him she felt a bit tired but all right. Not fuzzy headed at all. He led her to one of the couches and ask everyone to give her a bit of room.

Officer Stanford brought her a cup of water.

"Ladies. We are all glad to have Mrs. Westheimer back safe and sound." Humphrey smiled at her. "But please, refrain from asking her about her experience. This is still a police investigation, and we don't want her answers to influence your own. She has been told to only answer our questions, so please do not place her in an awkward position. We appreciate your cooperation."

Wanda sighed. Great.

Suddenly the door creaked open again. A handsome

young man in his mid-twenties, wearing a Scrub Oak police uniform, entered.

Thank the Lord.

"Todd!" Wanda's heart skated a triple axel worthy of the Olympic trials as she rushed over to him.

Humphrey's grin turned downward, and his bushy brows knitted to the center of his forehead.

Todd gave Wanda a small hug, briefly acknowledged Betty Sue and Evelyn, then turned his attention to the policeman gawking at him. He took four confident strides toward him, hand extended.

"Sergeant, I'm Officer Todd Martin from the Scrub Oak, Texas police department."

"So, I see." Humphrey eyed the town patch on Todd's left sleeve.

Wanda sucked in her breath. She detected in his tone a silent question asking why Todd would be on his turf.

Todd motioned toward Wanda. "Mrs. Warner is my aunt. She called me yesterday after being shaken up upon finding Mrs. Westheimer. I have driven over to be her advocate. If she has yet to be interviewed, I would appreciate being present. Ditto for Mrs. Simpson and Mrs. Jacobs who are also residents of the town where I serve." He glanced at Evelyn and Betty Sue. "I can explain in more detail in private."

The Louisiana policeman eyed him again then

grunted. He motioned for Todd to follow him to the porch. Officer Stanford followed, her thumbs tucked inside her utility belt.

Wanda felt every eye left in the living room on her. Now she knew how squirrels felt in the eyesight of an owl. Make that a cabin full of owls. Maybe she hadn't thought this through. She, Betty Sue, and Evelyn already stood out as Texans who drove quite a distance to attend a local retreat and she knew many of the women wondered why. Now her nephew shows up in uniform. Why had he not changed clothes?

Perhaps it wouldn't have mattered if he had. She'd still have to explain his presence.

She turned to face the ladies. "You see, I have been a consultant for the police in my town before and have helped solve several crimes. And seeing that I, along with my two friends and Olga, discovered evidence that may link to Sandie Hart's disappearance, well . . ." She stopped.

She noticed someone standing in the dining room, holding the coffee urn, head turned in her direction.

Flex.

His eyes narrowed to slits, then he frowned and pivoted to head into the kitchen.

Wanda started after him then halted after taking one step. No sense in following him. She had lost his trust. She could see it in his glare. Opportunity gone.

Wanda doubted anything she could say now would repair the damage.

Mary Jane stepped forward and laid her hand on Wanda's arm. "I think we are blessed to have these ladies here who have experience in dealing with the police." Her cheeks reddened as everyone's eyes focused on her. "Well, I mean in the area of crime investigation and such . . ." Her voice trailed off. She coughed just as the wham of the outside kitchen door closed with purposeful force.

Wanda heard the gravel crackle under stomped strides and through the double window she caught Flex heading for the van, shove the sliding side door shut, and then get into the driver's seat.

"That's not good." Evelyn's voice sounded beside her. "Did you get to speak with him?"

"Nope. And now I doubt he'll let me." Wanda gulped back her angst.

"Maybe he'd speak with Todd. They are closer in age, you know." Betty Sue grabbed her hand. "You saw Todd through his troubled teen years. Maybe if Flex knew that, well it might help him trust you more, right?"

Wanda gave Betty Sue a doubtful expression. "We need to get in touch with Brad before Flex does. Something tells me those two know more than they are letting on."

"I agree." Betty Sue sighed. "But Olga was his

contact. I'm not sure he'd speak with me again."

"Right." She searched the women for their friend and found her on the couch rubbing her forehead. "Let's go talk with her."

Evelyn grabbed Wanda's sleeve. "But the police said not to."

"Not to ask her about the assault last night. We can still talk with her."

Wanda figured from her two friends' faces, they thought she drew a very fine line, but they followed.

The three weaved through the cluster of ladies, who had begun to chat among themselves again. Wanda sat next to Olga, Betty Sue knelt in front of her, and Evelyn perched on the armrest. Wanda gently nudged her with her shoulder. "Hey, you had us worried. You okay?"

"Yeah. Still throbs a bit. I understand you found me. Thanks."

"No problem. We all three searched for you when you didn't return from speaking with Brad." She trailed the lad's name hoping Olga would pick up on the hint.

Her eyes narrowed for a split second then brightened. "Oh. Yes. I'd forgotten." She bobbed her head a few times then grimaced.

It must really hurt. Wanda waited. Only then did she realize it had been a while since she'd spotted Martha. Perhaps the police were speaking with her. No, wait. They had come to see Olga and . . . Wanda replayed the scene. Martha had definitely not been present. And Rachel had slipped out as well. Hmm. Well, lunch time would be approaching soon. Maybe they decided to prepare it themselves since the police were still conducting interviews.

Her mind returned to Olga's voice.

"I did call Brad, but I only got his voicemail. I started to leave him a message as I reached to get a note pad from the glovebox. You know, in case I wanted to write anything down. Then . . . bam." She shrugged. "Next thing I know they are wheeling me on a gurney into the ambulance and my head throbbed something fierce."

"Hmm. You didn't see anyone then?"

"Um, I am not sure . . ." She cast her eyes to the floor. Then she took a sudden breath and her eyes widened. "Oh. I need to speak with Officer Humphrey for a minute."

CHAPTER 26

Olga sat forward, her eyes raised as she searched the room.

Wanda sat back. "I see him. Through there." She pointed to the French doors leading to the screened-in porch. As she did, she noticed Todd slip back in and head into the dining room, probably for a cup of water from the pitchers that were always laid out.

Olga eyed the doors then turned back to them. "Thanks. Listen, my family wants me to go home and rest. So, I'm not staying. Sorry. I just came back to gather my things. My son is on the way. I'm not supposed to be driving even though its only five miles or so." She shrugged and rose to go speak with the police.

"What's up with her? She had a weird look on her face." Evelyn folded her arms over her chest.

Wanda shrugged. "I don't know but she seemed nervous to me. If she didn't get in touch with Brad, someone obviously made sure she wouldn't later on. Which means they knew she wanted to."

"You think that's why she seems nervous? Someone in here followed her and overheard her?" Evelyn glanced around the living room as if she expected the guilty party to raise their hand and confess.

Wanda skimmed the women as well. "Maybe, but who?" Unless Flex or George wandered around late at night. Wanda doubted it. Since almost everyone by that time were in their pjs, if one of the women had seen a man, she most likely would have screamed.

A few minutes later, Olga passed back through, her eyes to the floor.

"Olga. Hope you feel better quickly." Evelyn leapt from the cushion to shake her hand goodbye. Evelyn rarely was a hugger. "I've really enjoyed meeting you."

"Me, too." She touched her forehead and gave Evelyn a pained smile. "Mostly."

Betty Sue and Wanda waved goodbye to Olga as she edged toward the stairwell to head to her room. Rachel met her at the bottom rung, suitcase in hand. "Here, I think I packed everything. If not, I can drop it off later. And we'll get your car back to you as soon as the police says it's okay."

"Thank you, Rachel. How kind."

Wanda lifted her chin. So that's where she had been. But where was Martha? Wanda peered out the windows and then into the dining room but couldn't see her anywhere.

"No sense you trying to climb those stairs." She guided Olga to the door. "Now let's wait outside for Timothy. He drives a tan Honda as I recall, right?"

Olga waved goodbye to the ladies, most of whom now gazed in her direction. She received a chorus of best wishes in response.

Wanda smiled and mouthed her farewell. Then her focus landed onto Martha, now returning to the dining room with the coffee urn Flex had carried away in a hurry. Ah, that's where she'd been hiding. In the kitchen.

Had she and Flex argued? Is that why Wanda heard him slam the kitchen side door? Or had he simply been angry with Wanda for baiting him with the suggestion of writing for the paper? Perhaps both.

She thought back to the previous night. Olga had left the room to phone Brad while she and Betty Sue went to ask Martha about the crosswords. Martha had spoken with them in the living room for several minutes. Would she have seen Olga through the living room windows using her phone in the parking lot and then tattled to someone else, like Rachel or George, once she was back in her room? Come to think of it, Martha had seemed a bit in a hurry to cut her conversation with Wanda and Betty Sue short.

Even if she did, how would she have known that Olga called Brad? Unless, she had followed her and heard her start to leave a message . . . hmm. No, there wouldn't be time to notify anyone and have them arrive. Wanda doubted that Martha herself would have the wherewithal to whack anyone in the head. But she might be wrong about that. Martha did have a strong sense of control and duty, like her.

Wanda's eyes traveled to the woman's hand as she set the urn down and plugged it in. The knuckles appeared red and scraped. When had that happened?

"Ev. You were on breakfast duty. What did Martha do to her hand?"

"She said she scraped it on the wall of the cabin when she tripped on the stoop coming into the kitchen early this morning. But to be honest, it appeared older than that. I mean it wasn't bleeding. It'd already begun to scab over."

Really? Meaning it might have happened last night. She certainly didn't have the scratches when they spoke with her in the living room about the difference in the crosswords. Wanda would have noticed. Did her hand scrape across the top of Olga's car window or the car's chrome trim as she withdrew it from whacking her?

Wanda thought back to recall if Martha had held

her hands to cover her fingers or hidden them behind her last night when the police came. Her brain didn't bring any such images to mind.

Maybe Todd could discreetly discern if there were flecks of flesh along the car door's sash. Wanda rose and went to speak with him as he walked back toward the porch. Humphrey reentered through the French doors just as he approached.

"Mrs. Warner?" Humphrey called out and then noticed her standing. "If you please?"

Wanda glanced back at her friends and gave them a quick smile of reassurance. As she strolled across the room with every ounce of confidence she could muster, she couldn't help but feel like a leper in the Bible. The other women moved well out of the way as if they didn't wish to associate with her.

If Martha proved to be involved, would they shun Wanda even more for discovering that fact?

Julie B Cosgrove

CHAPTER 27

The expression on Todd's face warned her not to, but she couldn't help it. Wanda had to speak first as they sat down at the table on the porch—she and Todd on one side and Humphrey on the other.

"Officer Humphrey. I want to explain why Olga was in the parking lot and our conversation that led up to it."

He cocked his left eyebrow. "Exactly what I wanted to ask you, Mrs. Warner."

She shifted in the hard wooden chair then folded her hands across the card table. She walked him and Todd through the events of the evening before and explained her suspicions. Then she ended with the scrape on Martha's hand and Flex leaving in a huff.

Taking a deep breath—had she breathed at all during her monologue? —Wanda sat back and pursed her lips together.

Todd rubbed his forehead.

Humphrey's focus shifted between them for a minute, then he broke out into a hearty laugh. Officer Stanford shifted her stance behind him and chuckled as well.

"You're right, Martin. She is a handful."

Wanda opened her mouth to protest then shut it again before the temper her Irish ancestors placed in her DNA awakened like a banshee at moonrise.

"Mrs. Westheimer filled us in on her reasons for being alone in the dark, but I must say you have definitely given us a fuller picture."

"Did you check the car door for DNA?" The question spewed from her lips before her brain told her to hush up.

Todd groaned. "Aunt Wanda. Officer Humphrey is here to interview you, not vice versa." He flashed an apologetic grimace to the policeman.

Humphrey took a long sip of water then set the glass down before responding. Then he leaned forward. "Yes, ma'am. It is protocol to have a forensic team take samples at a crime scene. However, . . ." He twisted and spoke to the female officer. "See if they recovered anything from the car windows or doors."

She whispered an acknowledgement and pulled out her cell phone, then stepped to the other end of the porch.

"Reception in here is iffy. She might have to go outside . . ." Wanda started her sentence then clamped her lips again.

Humphrey blew a breath through his nose. "Okay, let me make sure I get this straight. You have an inkling that the members of the wrestling team might be involved, including Officer Mulligan's son, Aiden?"

So, they were father and son. That answered one question. "Yes, and maybe Martha who is a close friend of the caretakers Ruth and George whose grandson, Flex—"

"Got it." He held up his hand for her to stop talking.

For once, she complied.

He tapped a pen against the felt of the card table. "And the main reason would be because these team members went to school with the missing young lady, Sandie Hart?"

"Who recently broke up with Aiden Mulligan, one of the star players, the weekend the whole team had a sleepover up here."

His eyes widened then returned to a half scowl. "And this happened . . ."

"Third weekend in May from what I gather. Sandie broke up with him to date some college guy named Chad. My guess is that crushed Aiden, which stirred his friends into action."

"Wait." The policeman leaned forward. "You think they kidnapped Sandie?"

"I'm not sure. She may have planned to go off with this Chad guy and they found out about it and followed them. All I know is I have a gut feeling they know more than they are willing to discuss. And I think they know exactly who this Chad is and where he is. Find him and you may be able to find Sandie."

"Then why have they not come forward?" Todd joined in the conversation for the first time. "If they were concerned for her, wouldn't they want to yank her from his influence in hopes she'd return to Aiden who cares about her?"

Humphrey tippy-tapped his pen again. "He has a point. Though teenagers can get so over dramatic and secretive. They often don't use common sense. I know. I have two."

That familiar icy tingle hit Wanda. "Oh, and do they go to school with Sandie, too?"

The officer screeched his chair back and stood. He bent over the table and pointed his pen at Wanda's nose. "Now you've gone too far, lady."

Todd pressed his hand to Wanda's shoulder to keep her seated. "I am sure my aunt didn't mean to insinuate—"

Humphrey's nostrils flared. He stepped back, dropped the pen to the table surface, and rubbed a hand through his hair. "As a matter of fact, they go to a parochial boarding school in Baton Rouge. Not that it's any of your business." He sat down again.

A thick silence filled the room. Officer Stanford stepped forward and whispered in his ear. Humphrey gave her a nod. "Okay, thanks."

Wanda followed his eyes as they landed on her face again, but the fire in them had extinguished.

"This does not leave this room, got it?"

Todd and Wanda responded at the same time. "Yes, sir."

"Human blood traces were retrieved from the driver's side door. They do not match Mrs. Westheimer's DNA. However, they are from a male, not a female. And they appear older, with traces of motor oil. My guess is she had her car serviced recently. Mechanics often have scraped knuckles."

Wanda's cheeks heated. She gave the policeman a nod and folded her hands in her lap. Contriteness whispered in her soul to apologize to Martha the first chance she got.

"And now, Mrs. Warner."

She raised her head and gazed at Humphrey. "Yes, sir?"

"It is my turn to ask the questions, all right?"

She swallowed hard. In her peripheral vision she noticed Todd leaning back with one foot angled across his leg.

She bobbed her head and returned her gaze to her hands. When would she ever learn to keep her nose out of official police business? The names on her list of apologies increased, starting with her Lord for her prideful behavior . . . again.

CHAPTER 28

The rest of the interview droned on with Wanda answering in short sentences. On two occasions, Todd intervened politely to clarify what had been asked. Otherwise, he sat silently and absorbed everything she revealed. Wanda knew his thoughtful expression well enough to understand he filed each answer away in his brain to sort through later.

Finally, Office Humphrey scooted his chair legs back and rose. "Thank you, Mrs. Warner. You have been most cooperative."

Todd offered his hand to her elbow to help her rise.

"Officer Stanford, give me a few minutes to grab a cup of coffee then please ask Mrs. Simpson to come in. Officer Martin, do you wish to stay?"

"If you don't mind, sir. Simply as support. Mrs. Simpson would appreciate it, too, I believe."

"Very well."

Todd walked Wanda to the exit. "I'll catch up with you at lunch."

Wanda blinked back unshed tears. Humility rose in her throat. "Thank you for being here, Todd."

"No problem." He squeezed her elbow then opened the left French door wider for her to pass.

Evelyn and Betty Sue rushed to Wanda's side as she stepped back into the living room, thankful that the women had somewhat dispersed into small groups, so all eyes didn't land back upon her.

"Well?"

Wanda rubbed her lips together. "Humphrey is a gentleman, but he is also sharp as a tack. Just answer him honestly but don't offer more than necessary."

"You don't think he suspects one of us still, do you?"

Wanda grabbed her glass of water from the fireplace mantle and took a long gulp. Tepid now but it still quenched her dry throat. "I hope not. At first, I thought he might think we baited her and then when alone, one of us bludgeoned her. But if we were not the last people to be with Olga, who was?"

Evelyn thought for a moment. "And why did he, or she I suppose, whack her on the head and knock her out?"

"Exactly. It only makes sense that somebody didn't

want her talking to Brad Barton. Who and why?" Wanda thumped her fingers against her head. "Argh. I know I need to let this go and let the police handle it. Afterall, it is all speculation on my part."

Betty Sue gave her a wise nod, but Evelyn's face took on a perplexed expression. "What do you mean?"

"We can't be certain that the crossword puzzle clues are any more than that. Perhaps we stumbled upon the shoe by accident. No one led us there. And it might not be Sandie's. Brad did say a lot of girls got those type of socks on Valentine's Day."

"I suppose. But hers had apples, her favorite fruit. Not hearts or flowers. And pink, her favorite color. Seems fairly specific to me."

The tone in Evelyn's voice made Wanda wonder if she agreed or not. Wanda pressed further. "It may be the puzzle clues differed just as Martha stated, so not everyone would rush to the same location at once."

"Then why were ours different from the other odd numbered rooms?" Betty Sue moved closer.

Ah, so Betty Sue still had a tad bit of snoop-desire in her. Wanda tried not to smirk. "Because we were the last to register. Flex had to construct them at the last minute." Wanda plopped down in one of the couch cushions. "Look, we don't know if any of this has anything to do with Sandie's disappearance. It could have been a burglar casing cars at a secluded retreat center, seeing an older lady as a target, and getting spooked when he heard me coming around the corner."

Evelyn sat as well and leaned in as she lowered her voice. "But you don't think so, do you?"

Wanda peered into her friend's eyes. "No, do you two?"

Evelyn shook her head quickly. So did Betty Sue.

Evelyn chuckled. "That policeman got to you, didn't he?"

"Yes. I guess. And he will be calling you next, Betty Sue as soon as he gets a cup of coffee." She leaned back onto the cushions as well, but as she did the piece of paper rustled in her pocket. She pulled it out.

"What's that?" Betty Sue reached for it.

"I forgot to tell them. I found it behind that painting. The one with the deer overlooking the waterfall." She emphasized the words deer and waterfall.

Betty Sue's eyes widened as she obviously recalled the painting in their room. "Oh, my. I see."

Her friends' interest fueled her curiosity again. Wanda's gut simply told her she had not been on a bunny trail after all. It all had to fit together somehow, even if the painting didn't have an apple in it. *Oh well, Todd, I tried.*

Just then Officer Stanford called Betty Sue's name.

Wanda handed her the paper. "Here, show them this. Explain that I found it behind the painting, shoved it in my pocket, and in the confusion of Olga returning simply forgot to tell them."

"Then they will know we talked. And we aren't supposed to."

Sweet Betty Sue. She always followed the rules to the letter.

"It'll be okay. Trust me." She squeezed the paper into her friend's hand and watched her turn to walk toward the porch.

Then Evelyn's nose twitched. "What is that amazing aroma?"

Another attendee walked by and halted. "Chicken and Green Chile Casserole. Brenda's recipe." She indicated with her eyes for them to notice a thin, tall woman with red hair and an apron tied to her waist emerging from the kitchen into the dining area. "She often brings it to our church potlucks. It is really yummy."

Evelyn thanked her and rubbed her tongue across her lips.

Wanda, on the other hand, felt her stomach clench. She hoped it didn't turn out too spicy. Even though born and raised a Texan, her taste buds had always been wimpy. And she had heard these Louisiana folk loved spicy foods.

Besides, she rarely had a strong appetite when her brain swirled with what-if scenarios. Stomach juices rarely churned once her brain juices did.

"Wait, doesn't Betty Sue have lunch duty?" She looked at Evelyn. "I better go see if I can fill in for her since I have already been interrog . . . um, interviewed."

And hopefully corner Martha to apologize. She'd made a reckless, and wrong, assumption. Though Wanda didn't have an inkling about what she'd say, she knew she had to try. Maybe the lady had been influenced enough by the weekend lectures to show her a large pound of grace.

Wanda could only hope.

CHICKEN AND GREEN CHILE CASSEROLE

Ingredients:

- 3 pounds of chicken breast, cooked and finely chopped or shredded – Be sure to save the broth.
- 1 can of cream of mushroom soup
- 1 can of cream of chicken soup
- 4 ounce can of chopped green chiles, drained
- 1 teaspoon of chili powder
- 4 teaspoons of minced onion – I use yellow onions. You can use dehydrated onion flakes if you wish.

- 1/8 teaspoon of garlic powder – Too much will overpower the flavor.
- ¼ teaspoon of ground pepper.
- ½ teaspoon of tabasco sauce – Or Mexican hot sauce if desired.
- A 9 ounce bag of regular size corn chips – You'll want to munch on what you don't use.
- 8 ounces (one bag) of shredded cheddar cheese or Mexican blend cheese

Directions:

1. Preheat the oven to 350° F. Mix together the soups with one cup of the broth.

2. Spread corn chips in the bottom of a 9x13 casserole dish.

3. Blend the chicken and 4 ounces of the cheese together with the dry spices and onions. Layer one half across the chips.

4. Pour one half of the broth and soup mixture to evenly coat.

5. Repeat, then add the remaining 4 ounces of cheese to the top.

6. Bake at 350° F for 30 minutes.

7. Makes 6 servings.

Julie B Cosgrove

CHAPTER 29

Wanda didn't get a chance to sample the casserole, though. As she moved to join the buffet line Todd grabbed her arm.

"Hey, you need to come with me."

"What is it?" She didn't cotton to the expression on his face.

He shook his head and pulled her gently toward the entrance to the porch.

Evelyn pivoted, plate in hand, her whole face forming a silent question.

Wanda glanced back wide-eyed to convey her surprise then allowed Todd to lead her back to the interview room.

Betty Sue sat at the table sniffling. Her red-rimmed eyes met Wanda's.

"What's going on?" Wanda jerked away from

Todd's grip and rushed to hug her friend as she sat next to her.

Humphrey sat back, his arms folded over his toned-at-the-gym chest. The piece of paper from behind the deer painting lay unfolded on the card table. "Wanna explain why you were so eager to tell us everything . . . except this?"

Wanda wetted her lips. "I honestly forgot I had it in my pocket. I'd just discovered it when Olga came back, and then Todd arrived, and then—"

"—You decided to break the rules and discuss the case with your friend here and give it to her to show me." He slammed the legs of his chair to the floor again and peered into her face. "You do beat all, Mrs. Warner. I have half a mind to arrest you for withholding evidence and impeding an investigation."

Wanda sputtered. She stared at Todd, standing off to the side since she'd taken his chair. He returned her gaze with an arched eyebrow.

Betty Sue whimpered again.

The walls began to close inward. The room became a trap waiting to snatch her. She felt her heart pound a mantra inside her ears . . . don't speak, don't speak, don't . . . she ignored the warning.

Wanda shot to her feet and pointed her finger at the police officer's slightly crooked nose.

"How dare you. My friend has done nothing wrong.

Neither have I. We have cooperated every step of the way and let you know about everything we have gleaned." She twisted to Todd, her fingernails now digging tiny half circles into her palms. "Help us. That's why we called you."

He leaned against the wall and rubbed a small circle in his temple. "Aunt Wanda, this time you have gone way too far. Thank goodness you had the sense to bring this to us instead of traipsing off to some caves in this area and getting lost in one."

She lowered her eyes.

Todd let off a cynical chuckle. "Just as I thought. You had that plan in the back of your head, didn't you?"

He stepped away from the wall. "Sorry, Humphrey. She can be a handful, but she means well. Honestly. And Betty Sue, well, she is a kind-hearted, honest, good friend who tends to get sucked into my aunt's wake as she goes full steam ahead."

Betty Sue blew her nose. "I warned you not to get involved, Wanda. You know I did."

Why did the whole world hate her? Wanda blinked back the rising emotions stinging her eyes. All she wanted to do was help.

She slammed her fist to the table. "I can't help the fact that evidence lands at my feet, can I? You have to admit, Officer Humphrey, our crossword puzzle differed from everyone else's using the words trespass, doe, apple, and pour, which not only led us to find what appears to be Sandie's shoe and socks but also to a painting with a note taped to the back of it telling us to look in the cave."

She straightened her spine. "And, if you observe, the paper is not discolored and matches the ones on the notepads in the living room. The ink is a blue gel pen, like the ones we are using on the retreat. It only makes sense the note was written here and recently."

She stopped, took a breath, and slumped back into the chair.

Todd pressed his lips together but his eyes glimmered. Despite the fact he seemed irritated with her, she also sensed pride oozing into his facial expression. Yes, her observant skills, after years of solving word puzzles, still remained sharp as ever, even if she did say so herself.

Officer Stanford, who had been silent up to this point, whispered in Humphrey's ear, loud enough for Wanda to hear.

"Sir, perhaps if we took a small break. It seems they are serving lunch in there. These ladies may want to eat before it's all gone."

Humphrey's face lost some of the redness that had bloomed during Wanda's tirade. He repositioned in the chair. "Okay. Go get us all plates. Martin, do you mind helping her? And ask the other lady, um . . ." He glanced at the list. " . . . Mrs. Jacobs to join us as well."

Todd nodded and followed Stanford out of the room. Humphrey stood and went to drag two more chairs around the table. He remained silent.

Wanda and Betty Sue exchanged eye contact then sucked in a deep sigh simultaneously.

Wanda whispered that she was sorry.

Betty Sue lowered her eyes and nodded, then squeezed two of Wanda's fingers.

The sound of the mantle clock striking the hour echoed through the doorway into the suddenly still and stifling screened-in porch.

Then the room darkened, and a distant rumble sounded. Thunder.

The air smelled of damp soil. Ripples danced on the pond. A brisk breeze swirled some fallen leaves then flapped against the porch screen. Sure signs of rain approaching.

Not good. Rain would wash away evidence. Ruin any footprints in the gravel or dirt. Impede any search for Sandie.

Why, Lord? Wanda closed her eyes.

She had come on this retreat to rest, relax and rejuvenate. So far, none of these had been within her grasp. Instead, like the storm brewing outside, she had stirred up things . . . again.

Julie B Cosgrove

CHAPTER 30

The lights overhead flickered nanoseconds after a booming clap of thunder shook the cabin. The windows rattled. Several women squealed.

Wanda pressed her lips together so hard to keep from laughing at the stunned expressions on the policeman's face that they almost went numb. Seemed the big, stern cop could be spooked, too. The rumbles continued to roll into the distance as if laughing at its ability to make humans of all genders, ages, and sizes jolt.

Humphrey rose and pressed the walkie-talkie clipped next to his breastbone. "Jake, is forensics about done out there. All you-know-what is about to break loose."

Ah, so they had returned in the daylight to gather more evidence. Wanda wished she could be a bug on one of the windshields so she could observe what else, if anything, they retrieved to analyze.

"Yes, sir." We saw it moving in. They packed up about ten minutes ago. Said we'd get the report within four hours."

"Okay, find Stanford and have her help you wrap things up. I've got it handled in here."

Todd returned with two plates and set them down for Betty Sue and Wanda.

Wanda turned to Todd and whispered in his ear. "Report on what?"

The only response she received was a daggered glare. Then he grabbed another chair and pulled it next to her.

She edged back in her chair.

Evelyn entered with her half-eaten plate of food then sat next to her after noticing Betty Sue's red rimmed eyes. "What's going on?"

Wanda shrugged. "They are kinda upset about us gathering evidence. Something about impeding their investigation."

"What? We've done nothing but help them. Of all things holy . . ." she harumphed and folded her arms.

Todd stretched his torso toward Wanda and put his finger to his lips. Then he left again to retrieve a plate of food for himself and Officer Humphrey.

Humphrey walked back toward them, still speaking

to Jake, whoever he was. "Okay. Head on out, then and take Black with you. Mulligan will probably need help on the highways. People drive crazy in this stuff."

He returned to his chair and focused on the new addition to the group. "Mrs. Jacobs, I presume."

"Exactly, my dear fellow." She gave him a smirk.

Wanda wasn't sure if Evelyn referred to Sherlock Holmes' Watson or Dr. Livingston's Stanley in her cryptic response. But from the stone-cold face of Officer Humphrey, she surmised he didn't find her response amusing.

Betty Sue must have kicked her shin because Evelyn frowned at her and shifted in her chair.

Humphrey opened his mouth but whatever he meant to say became lost in another huge clap of thunder. Then loud swishes of rain began to pour off the roof, encasing them inside a waterfall. The drops pelted the ground, drowning out all other sounds.

His scowl turned into one of exasperation. Obviously, the man didn't care for thunderstorms. Wanda felt exhilarated by them, but then again, she didn't have to be on call to rescue people from swelling creeks or overturned vehicles.

Just as Todd appeared with their two lunches, Humphrey told them all to eat then return to the living room. The rain might filter through the screens and get them all wet if the winds continued.

Everyone chewed in silence for several minutes. Betty Sue, Wanda, and Evelyn exchanged glances now and then, but mostly kept their eyes on their plates. Todd gobbled his meal down, along with two rolls. Poor guy, maybe he never ate breakfast. Humphrey relaxed a little and mumbled that these ladies sure knew how to cook.

At least the dish didn't burn her tongue or cause excess acid in Wanda's tummy. In fact, it tasted quite good. Maybe she'd make it sometime as a potluck at her church.

After they finished, Todd rose and pulled out Wanda's chair, then Betty Sue's. Humphrey wiped his mouth and followed suit with the gentlemanly gesture for Evelyn. "I've decided not to interview you, ma'am. My guess is your version wouldn't differ from theirs anyway."

Then he gathered up his papers and phone and swaggered through the door. Todd motioned for the ladies to follow.

Their procession reminded Wanda of a scene from an 18th century prison movie. She almost expected to see Mary Jane clutching her Bible and reading the Lord's Prayer as a black hooded Flex prepared the guillotine. Wanda rubbed her temples. Man, she must be tired to conjure up such an image. Best keep it to herself.

A bolt of lightning whitened the room, then all went still, and dark.

Martha called out above the squeals. "The generator will kick on in a minute. And we have flashlights and hurricane lanterns in the kitchen to illuminate your bedrooms. Besides many of you have flashlight apps on your phones, right? No worries, ladies. God is with us."

Stanford appeared, her shoulders and hair dripping wet, and asked Humphrey if she could help distribute the lanterns to any on the second floor already and he nodded approval. Then he turned to Wanda, Betty Sue, and Evelyn. "Are you three staying in the same room?"

Wanda responded that they were.

"May we intrude on your space, ladies? There are still a few things we need to discuss in private."

Wanda glanced at Evelyn and Betty Sue who each gave her a small shrug. "Okay. But the only things to sit on are our three beds."

"We'll make do. Martin, I'd like you to be there as well. And it will all be recorded so everything will be above board. Shall we?" He extended his hand.

Todd raised his eyebrows at Wanda, indicating she should lead the way. He flicked on the flashlight app on his phone and shined it toward the staircase.

Now why didn't I think of that? Wanda clicked on her app as well.

When they entered their room, the lights flickered back on, and the faint whir of the generator could be heard.

"Praise the Lord." Betty Sue sighed under her breath. Wanda patted her back. At the ripe old age of sixty-three, Betty Sue still slept with a nightlight on in her bedroom. Darkness always gave her the creeps.

Humphrey gestured for the three ladies to sit on the bed to the far right. He laid all his things out on the middle bed and then asked Todd to join him perched on the edge of the third bed facing the ladies.

Wanda figured he had interviewed many people in their homes and hospital rooms and only God knew where else. There must've been a propriety protocol to follow. Even so, she had one more reason to be thankful for her nephew's presence. And as soon as Todd spoke, she found yet another.

He raised his voice a few notches to be heard over the rain pelting the tin roof above them. "Sir, I know these ladies, and they have been instrumental in gathering information which led to solving several crimes in our hometown, including one that had been cold for decades. They don't mean to impede, only to assist. My aunt," he nodded toward Wanda, "is responsible for organizing a neighborhood watch force in our community and it has greatly enhanced our force's ability to serve and protect. She even received an accommodation from our mayor."

Humphrey shot Wanda a look then returned his

attention to Todd.

He finished with an apologetic expression. "They've developed keen eyes, and each have a deep sense of community and justice. It's simply what they do. They meant no offense."

The Louisianan policeman ran his hand through his hair again. "Okay. Ladies, forgive me if I have been gruff. Gotta a lot of pressure on me to find this teenage girl. Every hour this drags on means more breathing down my neck from the parents, the community and even the governor now."

"The let's then pool our resources and go over everything one more time pertaining to her disappearance." Wanda opened her hands wide as if to offer a truce.

"What about Olga?" Evelyn blurted it out then placed her hand to her mouth when she noticed his eyes narrow. "Sorry. You were saying, sir?"

"Start at the beginning and explain again how you concluded that these crossword answers might be connected to the disappearance of Miss Hart."

The three ladies walked him through their time at the retreat. They explained the puzzles, and why they surmised theirs had been made differently.

Humphrey acted attentive and asked questions in a mild manner only when he wanted clarification. His attitude had definitely softened. Wanda wondered if

Todd had been instrumental in the shift or if it was a ploy to gain their trust. She decided to cooperate fully as she continued to speak for her friends as well. Ten minutes later, she concluded.

"And that's when I noticed the deer painting with the note taped to the back of it. Pretty cliché, I have to admit." Wanda pointed to the creased piece of paper with the printed message.

"I see. So now you believe the crossword answers were supposed to lead you to this painting and not the brook?"

"Hadn't quite worked it out yet. Maybe the painting was supposed to be the clue to lead us to the waterfall. Is there a cave nearby it? I mean, we have caves in Texas along the I35 fault line but are there any here in northern Louisiana?"

Humphrey leaned back on his hands. "Actually, there are. Everyone around here knows where they are. We monitor them because the kids use them to do stuff their parents and the law might frown upon. Also, vagrants camp out in a few."

Todd scooted forward in order to catch the police officer's attention. "So, it is feasible that Sandie might know where one is near this property since she hung out with the wrestling team. She could have broken away from her captor and escaped down the brook to find it."

"If she was kidnapped. We have no indication to

suspect she has been. There has been no ransom note, no phone calls. We are treating it as a runaway."

"Wait. What about the bloody sock?" Wanda's voice squeaked with emotion. She cleared her throat and started again. "We know Aiden Mulligan gave her a pair with the same pink apple design for Valentine's. We gave them to Officer Mulligan."

"Them?"

"Yes, the blood-stained sock, along with the shoe, and the other sock Olga and Evelyn found further down the creek." Hadn't they gone over this before? Why did the policeman's face go blank? "We don't know Sandie's shoe or sock size, and we learned these types of socks became very popular around Valentines, but . . ."

Humphrey's complexion lost color. "Excuse me a minute." He rose and left the room.

The three ladies exchanged inquisitive glances.

Todd pressed his hands to his knees. "Something tells me Aiden's dad has not been completely forthcoming about his connection to this whole thing."

Julie B Cosgrove

CHAPTER 31

The pattering on the roof began to slow in intensity and the rumbles sounded more and more distant. The four Texans sat in the room and waited but Humphrey didn't return. Todd raised his wrist to view his watch. "It's been a half hour. Are we to stay put or leave?"

"You tell us." Evelyn harumphed. "I feel like a trapped rat. Wonder what the other ladies are doing."

"Probably have started the lecture we were supposed to have this morning." Betty Sue rose and jutted her chin. "Well, he didn't tell us to stay here. I'm thirsty. Anyone else want anything to drink?"

"Let's all go grab something." Wanda scooted off the bed and headed for the hallway.

When they arrived at the stairs, they heard Mary Jane's presentation tone of voice. Wanda signaled for the rest to wait then she tiptoed down and peered around the landing. Sure enough, the session had started, and the ladies gathered in a semi-circle around the whiteboard, many with Bibles opened on their laps.

Wanda ducked and slipped back up the stairs. "We better go out the side door down to the kitchen. I think the rain has stopped enough."

The four light-footed down the hall to the outside staircase.

Betty Sue let out a nervous giggle as she descended the steps. "I feel like a truant."

Todd snickered. "It's okay. If the principal snags you by the ear, I will come to your aid."

She blushed. "Don't you dare."

Then he must have realized his faux pas considering Betty Sue and ex-principal Fred had officially become an item over the past few months. His hand shot to cover his mouth.

Wanda and Evelyn chuckled as well.

They entered the kitchen. Rachel and Martha jolted and spun around.

"Oh, dear. Ya'll scared us half out of our skin." Martha pressed her palm to her heart. "Why aren't you with the group?"

"We were still being interviewed by Officer Humphrey. Then he left the room, and we kept sitting there expecting him to return." Wanda grabbed a glass and headed to the industrial refrigerator.

"But he never did. So, we came down to get a drink of water." Betty Sue tiptoed to the drainer and took a glass as well. Then she handed two more to Todd and Evelyn.

Todd extended his hand. "Were we formally introduced? I am Todd Martin, Wanda's nephew."

Rachel eyed his uniform. "Rachel McDavid. Proprietor. And this is Martha Raymond who has coordinated this retreat."

"Please to meet you, ladies."

"Exactly why are you here, Officer Martin?" Rachel fiddled with her necklace chain.

"Aunt Wanda became upset over finding Mrs. Westheimer. She phoned me last night, and I told her I would drive over after I got off shift to console her." His cheeks took on a deeper pink hue. "We're very close. She practically raised me."

"I see." Rachel released her stare and untied her apron. "There are some chocolate chip cookies left, if you want any."

Martha picked up on the cue and grabbed the bakery box from the counter. Todd snatched a paper napkin and used it to choose one. He handed them out one by one to the women then picked one for himself and bit into it. "Mm. Quite delicious. Thanks."

Then he leaned against the steel rolling cart in the center of the kitchen. "Tell me about the caves in this area."

Wanda bit into her cookie to hide her grin.

"Well, there is one on our property about fifty yards from the little waterfall. Why?" Rachel's hand reached for her necklace again.

"Do you know why anyone would leave a note taped to the back of the deer painting by the fireplace wall that would say to look in the cave?"

Martha and Rachel shared stares. Then Rachel's shoulders relaxed. "Oh my. That must be from when the boys were here on their sleepover. George, my husband, and I put together a little Scavenger Hunt for them. It's kinda a tradition. We do it all the time for the grandkids. That's what made us think of doing the crossword puzzle ones for the ladies."

"Then what was in the cave?" Todd took a step toward her.

She inched back. "I don't rightly know. Probably the next clue. Anyway, it ended up with a bonfire and s'mores in the back field by the brook." She let off a little snicker. "Now if you excuse me. I must get back up the hill to our home now that the rainstorm has ended."

She glanced at Martha and grabbed her car keys.

Todd raised his voice a tad to regain her attention. "Your husband is a retired forensic specialist, no?"

Rachel stopped and then pivoted back to him. "He

is." Her answer ended in a questioning lilt.

"Good friends with Office Mulligan he is, I guess? I mean considering Mulligan's son and your grandson are on the wrestling team together."

"We know them, of course. Have done quite a few pep rally activities and fundraisers for the team together over the years. Why?"

"Just associating the names. I think our force might have sent some evidence to Shreveport a while back." Todd gave her a soft grin.

Rachel returned his smile. "Well, my husband is well known. So, it doesn't surprise me."

"Yes, I am sure he has been invaluable on many cases. Especially locally. Does he still retain a lab even though he is retired?"

"Oh, not really. Well, I mean he still has some stuff in what used to be maid's quarters by the garage. I catch him in there piddling around when he should be mowing the lawn." With a lilting chuckle, she left.

Wanda looked to the floor and took another bite. The lad didn't actually lie. Yet he had gained the woman's trust enough to glean some important answers.

Martha folded a dish towel. "Well, I'm going to join the ladies. Are you three coming?"

Wanda and her friends exchanged eye contact.

Todd spoke up. "I think we need to locate Officer Humphrey and make sure he has finished interviewing them."

Martha clucked her teeth. "I imagine so. He left a good ten minutes ago. See you in a minute, then? Not you, Officer Martin. Women only, you see. But you can find some way to amuse yourself I'm sure. Maybe wander down by the pond?" She eyed each of the ladies and waltzed out of the kitchen toward the dining area and living room.

Evelyn's mouth flew open. "Wow. She sure told us."

Wanda hiked her hands to her hips. "Well, I'll be . . ."

Betty Sue spit out the drink of water in her mouth and laughed into her fist.

Todd scratched his head. "This gets more and more interesting."

"What do we do now, Todd?" Wanda turned to him as he snatched another cookie.

He chewed for a moment before responding. "I have a sneaky feeling that Mulligan gave George the socks and had him run a forensic test on them. That is why Humphrey didn't know about them."

"How would George know Sandie's DNA?"

"Easy, Aunt Wanda. From Aiden. I imagine he has some memorabilia from her. A love note that she may have sealed with a swipe of her tongue. Maybe even a lock of hair."

"So, you think the team is involved?"

"I didn't say that. In fact, Sandie's DNA may not be necessary at all. If he is worth his reputation he would have contacted her family doctor to find out her blood type. Then see if that matched the stains on the sock. Knowing she owned such a pair may be proof enough."

"Oh, of course. Aiden gave them to her." Wanda crossed her arms.

"But I am guessing George may want it for process of elimination." He dusted the crumbs from his hands on his pants. "I do think some of the team may know what happened to her."

"Todd. What are you thinking?" Wanda stared into his face and tried not to notice the slight chocolate smear next to the corner of his mouth lest she dab it with her finger and embarrass the heck out of him.

"Wait." Evelyn drew closer. "You think some of the wrestling team knows where she is, don't you, Todd?"

"I imagine so. Teenagers stick close together, you know. When one is hurt, they all rally. If Sandie broke up with Aiden, my guess is his teammates might seek revenge on the college dude who pulled her away. Maybe even give him a little lesson about dating high school juniors." He gave them a smirk. "Ever consider the blood on the sock may not be hers? That she removed her shoe and used her sock to dab a split lip or bloody nose?"

No, Wanda's brain had never conjured up that scenario. Not at all. But then, unlike her nephew, she had never been a teenaged boy.

CHAPTER 32

Wanda shook her head in amazement. Her nephew did have smarts. Acting more like detective material every day. Maybe he'd consider taking the courses to become one. Then the two of them . . . She blinked from that dream at the sound of Evelyn's voice.

"You think George might use the blood to do a DNA trace to discover who this Chad dude is, right?" Evelyn nudged Todd in the arm.

"It's a possibility. But maybe not. No one gives their DNA voluntarily to the police when they get a driver's license. If these kids have never been in trouble, then probably theirs is not on record. And if they are under eighteen, their parents can refuse their being tested."

Evelyn harumphed. "How convenient."

"As we interviewed the other ladies, Officer

Humphrey seemed pretty adamant that Sandie is not a kidnapping victim. He steered away from all comments about her. That means she ran off voluntarily, and my guess is it was to have a weekend tryst with her new college boyfriend."

"The snake." Betty Sue tskd.

Todd laughed and pulled out his phone. "Betty Sue, we don't know this girl. She may not be all that innocent."

"We already figured that out from her latest social media posts." Wanda scoffed. "This Chad guy definitely has changed her views on life."

"I'd like to see some of her comments. Can you pull them up again?"

"If I can get bars on my phone. The parking lot is the best hotspot."

Todd glanced at his aunt. "Ah. Which is why Olga went out there to phone one of the wrestling team members. Why did she want to speak with him again?"

"Brad Barton goes to her church. Olga knows his family. She thought he might have some insight about the breakup and Aiden's demeanor and also to see if he might know something about this Chad dude. She had spoken to him earlier but wanted to talk with him again."

"And you ladies believe someone didn't want her chatting with Brad a second time. That is why she got conked."

"Seems the most logical." Wanda scrunched her mouth to one side.

"I agree, though suddenly Humphrey seems more concerned about Sandie. Maybe because your friend Olga appears to be okay."

"He did say people were breathing down his neck." Betty Sue lifted her finger to make her point.

Wanda snapped hers. "Or he thinks finding Sandie will answer some questions about why Olga was attacked."

"Could be, Aunt Wanda. Which means someone overheard you ladies discussing it and followed her outside."

"But we were in our room behind closed doors. That is what freaks us out." Betty Sue rubbed her arms. "How did they hear us? Was somebody listening through the door?"

Todd glanced up at the air vent above the spot where Martha and Rachel had stood in the kitchen rolling silverware into paper napkins.

"Aunt Wanda. Do me a favor. Go back into your room and have a conversation with yourself."

She felt her brainwaves kick in. "You think our conversations filtered through the vent?"

"Your room is above here, isn't it?"

The three ladies stared at each other for a moment.

Evelyn winked. "I'll do it." She dashed out the side door.

A few minutes later they heard her voice in an echo. "Here I am talking to myself. La, de, da."

Todd found a broom and raised the handle to the cedar ceiling. He tapped the planks three times.

Three taps resounded back. Then Wanda heard Evelyn's footsteps on the stairs as she dashed down.

"Well?" She stopped, slightly out of breath.

Todd's lips moved into a sly grin. "We heard you loud and clear. Which means someone else could have as well."

Wanda narrowed her eyes. "I wonder which boys had that room the weekend of the sleepover? Could Rachel and George have overheard about Sandie's breakup with Aiden and planned a revenge?"

Todd blew out his breath. "Interesting if we could find out. It might help us learn about Sandie. Though I am not sure if that would help us in finding Olga's assailant. In fact, I am not convinced any of the wrestling team had anything to do with Olga's incident."

"Really?" Wanda stared at him. Why would Todd say such a thing? It seemed to her all the clues pointed directly at them.

"Yes. I also wonder how much Rachel and Martha heard of our discussion with Officer Humphrey earlier."

He pointed back to the vent.

"But Todd. They acted startled when we four entered the kitchen."

"True, Aunt Wanda. The key word is *acted*."

"Oh. I get it." Betty Sue's eyes lit brighter. "They only pretended so we wouldn't guess they eavesdropped, right?"

Todd's mouth curved up on one side. "Exactly. In my experience, when someone covers up something it usually means they don't want you to know what that something is."

"Wonder what else they've heard? Particularly last night." Evelyn sniffed. "We only assumed Martha went back to bed after we chatted with her."

Evelyn's comment sent Wanda's grey cells into overdrive. "Or what Martha may have heard *before* you both went to find her, when we all were figuring out the differences in the puzzles."

"Maybe Martha came into the kitchen to get a drink of water and overheard us and heard about the call Olga was about to make." Betty Sue raised her hand to her mouth.

"Then she dashed back into her room knowing we were headed down to chat with her about the crossword puzzles." Wanda eyed the three of them with a nod.

Evelyn pointed at her. "Yes. And before that, she told Rachel or George about Olga trying to reach Brad and how it might implicate Flex who is Aiden's friend."

"And either they stopped Olga or found someone else to do it." Wanda high-fived her friends. "Which means now Martha's afraid to come forward because it would make her an accessory." She focused back onto Todd. "Could that be it?"

Todd set his glass in the sink. "All good questions. Let's see if we can get someone to give us the answers."

CHAPTER 33

Wanda expected Todd to track down Martha. But he didn't. Instead, he pulled out a business card and punched the number into his phone.

She faintly heard it ring then a male voice answer.

Todd raised it to his ear. "Hi, can we meet? Oh, you were? Okay. Sure." He started to walk toward the kitchen side door. "Yeah, I can find it. Be there in ten."

"Where?" Wanda rushed after him.

He pocketed his phone then raised his eyes and scanned their faces. "Ladies, let me and the West Monroe police force handle things from here on out, okay? I'll be in touch." His eyes traveled to the door leading into the dining area and living room. "Go, enjoy the rest of your retreat. That is why you paid good money to come, right?"

His hand reached for the outside door handle, but

Wanda grabbed it first. "Why are you dismissing us like toddlers you pat on the head and tell to go outside and play while the grownups talk. Huh?"

She heard his deep sigh as he laid his hands on her shoulders. "Aunt Wanda. This isn't Scrub Oak. And even if it was, I wouldn't want you involved any further. Nor your friends. I don't need any of you getting the same treatment Olga did."

"But . . ."

His tone became sterner. "Officer Humphrey just told me he has information he wants to share with me. Combined with what we have just learned here, I think he and I can solve this case and probably bring Sandie home safely. Let us take things from here."

He kissed her cheek and left.

Wanda turned to her friends whose mouths resembled baby birds waiting to be fed.

"Well, you heard the man. I wish he'd told me where he was going and who he was meeting, but there it is." She shrugged. "We have been dismissed."

"Well, Todd was right." Betty Sue tilted her head. "We came here for the retreat. So, let's retreat… to the living room."

"As if I can concentrate on anything Mary Jane says right now." Wanda huffed as she headed to the door.

Betty Sue hooked her arm through Wanda's elbow. "Maybe we'll simply have to give her some grace."

Wanda's pout morphed into a semi smile. "Yeah, okay. No sense hanging out in here. Todd ate the last chocolate chip cookie anyway."

Evelyn chuckled. "Let's go."

As they slipped into the living room and found a place at the back, Wanda noticed Martha's eyes narrow onto them. Her mouth pressed into almost a white line between her cheek bones.

Betty Sue must have noticed the icy stare as well because she put on her sweet little ol' Betty Sue Southern lady grin.

Martha immediately returned her attention to Mary Jane.

Wanda swallowed the thought begging to erupt from her throat. What was Martha's deal anyway? She might simply be perturbed that her retreat, which she'd spent weeks planning, had been interrupted by these snoopy strangers from Scrub Oak who then involved one of the Louisiana ladies in their shenanigans. But something in the back of her brain told her differently.

She drowned out Mary Jane's voice and thought back to all Todd had mentioned in the kitchen.

The blood may be Chad's.

Aiden' teammates may have sought revenge on him for stealing Sandie away.

She may have used her sock to treat his wound, dabbing it in the cool stream.

The clue about the cave could have been left there from the lock in, or even before if Rachel's explanation could be believed. Or not.

One way to find out.

Find the cave.

All Wanda had to do was figure out how to slip out unnoticed, so she had time to locate it before dark. That is if Todd hadn't returned by then.

Was he still with Humphrey or could he be with Mulligan by now? How she wished she could have gone with him. Even just sat in the precinct's waiting room or around the corner while he talked to the other officers, though she'd never heard of a "Take your aunt to work" day.

Oohh, she itched to find out what was going on. She concentrated as hard as she could and sent brain vibes to Mary Jane to stop and take a ten-minute break.

Mary Jane suddenly capped her marker and set it near the white board. She glanced at Wanda then blinked before closing her Bible.

"Ladies, it is nearly three. Let's take a break, get refreshments, then resume in fifteen minutes, okay?"

Martha's face paled. Obviously, she had not planned for this at all. She rushed from the room, grabbing two of the other women on the way to help her in the kitchen.

Wanda sat back and grinned. "Well, I'll be. Thank,

you, Lord."

Julie B Cosgrove

Chapter 34

Wanda slipped out the front door. Even though residual rain clouds covered most of the sky, a sliver of afternoon sunlight shined down enough to illuminate the landscape. Between its glow and her memory, she easily traversed the field to the brook again. The tall cyprus trees made the bank down to the water too dark to navigate under the cloud cover, so she pulled out her phone and turned on her flashlight app. The last thing she needed was to take a tumble.

Now where would the cave be? Didn't Rachel say it was downstream from the waterfall? It had to be on the McDavid's land, then. The fence line ran along the top of the far bank, and it seemed steeper and rockier. Probably the cave lay on the other side of the brook, which meant she'd have to wade across.

She crouched to take off her shoes and socks, then

waved the phone app's beam over the rocks. Near the spot she recalled seeing the shoe, she noticed the water had risen due to the rain, but she could still see the tips of the riverbed stones. Shouldn't be too difficult.

With her shoes in one hand and her phone in the other, she extended her arms like a tightrope walker would. Wanda stuck her big toe into the stream. The rain had definitely cooled the current and it rushed more swiftly around her ankles as she stepped in.

Steadying her balance for a moment, she strode to the next rock, then the next. So far so good. The ripples pulled at her feet but not enough to make her lose her balance. After a few more steps, she reached the muddy bank on the other side.

She found a cypress branch to sit on, brushed the riverbank's leaves and mud from her bare feet, and pulled her footwear back on. Then she picked up her phone and used it to cast a beam of light across the ridge. Cypress limbs, grass tufts, and a few vines camouflaged the landscape, but she couldn't detect any dark holes that might be the entrance to a cave.

That left her two choices. Go back or continue to search. She brushed off her pants and headed further downstream. The rush of the swollen brook over the rocks became a white noise shutting out any other sounds. Almost lulling.

Should she call out Sandie's name? Would she be

lying injured in the cave, or would it only endanger her if her captor lay in wait? She may not hear Wanda's voice above the current anyway.

Wanda chose to remain silent and scanned the hillside. Her eyes had adjusted to the semidarkness better, but all the vegetation still made any indentations difficult to view.

A new thought caused her to stop. Why did she think the cave would be by the riverbed? It could be anywhere on the property. Rachel had said it lay below the waterfall, but she didn't say it opened up onto the bank. Just because the painting showed a deer by a waterfall didn't mean anything. Not knowing how far downstream she had traveled, Wanda couldn't determine if she trespassed onto someone else's property yet or not. Maybe she should move further inland on the other side and search in the field.

"No. Sandie definitely came this way because they found her other sock down here." She hissed to herself as if speaking out loud would make her brain hear her better. The cave had to be close by the brook.

Glancing around, she noticed the shadows deepening. Her phone told her she had been gone twenty minutes. Would anyone notice she had not returned after the break? Surely Betty Sue and Evelyn would. She chided herself for not letting them know her plan. Why had she headed out on her own?

She shoved the growing frustration down and continued to traipse over the bank careful to set each foot down on a sure surface. Determination to locate the cave, and possibly the girl, pushed her onward.

Something different caught her eye. She bent and twisted to view up the bank at a spot where the grass and vines parted. The cave? As she stretched a tad more to get a better view, Wanda's foot slipped in the mud, and it began to slide down toward the brook.

Wanda had never attempted the splits in her life, but her body tried it anyway. Her balance wobbled as her leg stretched out behind her and pulled her muscles. A pain shot up her leg into her rear-end and her back buckled.

Down she slid, her hands grabbing for anything to stop her fall. She felt herself heading sideways then crack. Her head contacted something very hard and immovable.

Sharp pain shot across her skull as a hot tingling cascaded down to her neck. Dizziness swirled the landscape around her as she rolled over onto her back, one leg underneath her and the other angled upward. Her right ankle throbbed. Her shoulder blade shot out in agony when she tried to move.

The leaves rustled as a strong breeze whipped down the stream and a flash of lightning zapped across the sky. Above her, the clouds began to rumble again as they closed off the last rays of sunlight trying to pierce through the cypress limbs.

Oh, great. Another round of thunderstorms. And here she lay—on her back with a throbbing foot, injured shoulder, and a dizzy head. And no one knew where she had gone.

Her lips quivered as she blinked against the raindrops dampening her face. "Dear Lord. Help me. Forgive me for my foolish need to rush ahead and not think."

She gulped back the panic threatening to envelop her. Quote Scripture. Someone had told her that whenever fear crept into her soul, verses from the Bible could be calming.

There in the rain, all else drowned out by the rush of the rising water which now lapped at her hair, Wanda grabbed for anything she could recall. Part of Psalm 23 broke through. She repeated it over and over.

"I will fear no evil for you, O Lord, are with me."

Please, don't let me drown.

Julie B Cosgrove

CHAPTER 35

A pair of hands pressed onto her shoulders. Wanda blinked through the bangs matted to her eyebrows and peered into the face of a young girl. Her cheeks were sculptured around wide, soft eyes. Her blond hair lay like a wet cloak over her shoulders. A thin gold chain dangled from her neck with an apple-shaped pendant at the end.

"Sandie?" Wanda's words wobbled in her throat.

"Yes." She cocked her head. "Who are you? Are you okay?"

Wanda tried to move, then her shoulder and head reminded her it wouldn't be a great idea. She let out a groan. "No, I don't think I am."

"The water is rising. We need to get you higher up. And dry."

Sandie shifted and wrapped her arm around

Wanda's back. "Here, can you sit up?"

Wanda felt the young girl's strength bend her torso. Her shoulder complained and her head swam for a moment. "Wait. Stop. I hit my head and I'm dizzy. My shoulder hurts, too."

"Oh, okay. Which one?"

"Left."

Sandie repositioned her weight so Wanda could lean against her. "Can you stand?"

Wanda shook her head and then regretted it. She answered through the stabbing pain. "I don't think so. I twisted my ankle, too."

"Can you hobble?"

Wanda gazed into the innocent face wanting to help her. "Let's try."

Relying on youthful stamina to assist her, Wanda gingerly rose up and let the girl's body balance her own. They wobbled several steps then Wanda begged her to stop.

"I know you are in pain, but we need to get out of the rain. There is a cave just a few more feet away. Let's go. You can do it."

The girl's tone resembled a cheerleader urging her team to score the final touchdown. Wanda sucked in a long breath. "Okay. Go."

The two stumbled and strode. Together they slowly traversed the small hill to the cave's entrance. Wanda ducked and hobbled inside, then scooted onto her rear and pulled herself against the stony wall. Her lungs burned from the effort and her breaths came quick and shallow, but she'd done it.

Sandie scrambled beside her and covered her with an unzipped sleeping bag. She tucked it around Wanda as if putting a small child to bed. "There, that'll keep you warmer."

"Thanks . . . Sandie . . . I . . . appreciate it." Her breathing continued to rasp.

"No worries. I'm sorry. Do I know you? I recall seeing you yesterday, but those policemen and George came by, so I hid again."

Aw, so that's why Wanda had sensed someone watching her. "Nope. You don't. Name's Wanda." As her lungs began to calm, she told Sandie briefly why she knew her and how she had ended up at the brook.

Sandie chuckled. "I wondered where my other shoe had gone." She held up a single one.

"Everyone is looking for you. What happened?"

The girl scooted closer and raised her knees to her chin. "I've been so, so stupid."

Wanda reached out and took one of the girl's hands. It felt as soft as a satin glove. "We all do stupid things we regret. It's called being human. But we have a forgiving God who shows grace. You are proof."

"I am?"

"I was stupid enough to try and find your cave on my own on a stormy afternoon. God sent you to rescue me. So, see? He thinks good of you. He's been watching over you and used you to help me."

"Gosh, you think? I figured He'd be angry with me. I've broken a lot of rules." She sniffed as she dabbed her eyes. "I heard you scream. I wasn't sure if it might be my friend, Ginger or not. Then I saw you lying there . . ."

"And you made the decision to help me. You have a good heart, Sandie."

"Do I? My boyfriend and I had this huge fight. Right after prom night. He's a senior and I'm a junior. He's heading off to college at LSU soon on a wrestling scholarship and . . ." Her voice shook.

"Right. I get it."

"He hurt me so bad. Then I heard his friends say I broke up with him! I guess I wanted to hurt him back. I snuck out and went to this party. This college guy started to hit on me." She turned toward Wanda. "I knew Brad and Flex were there and saw me. I only wanted to make Aiden jealous. So, I played along and agreed to leave with him. And we had a really great time. He was sweet, and gentlemanly . . ."

She wiped the tears off her cheeks again. "We dated for several weeks. He really opened my eyes to the world. He was so smart, and knowledgeable, being a college guy. I was in awe of him. He persuaded me to meet him by the lake. We arranged it all. I had my parents' permission to go with this group, so then I'd sneak off and find him."

"Did he show?"

"Yeah, with a backpack and sleeping bag. That should have set off alarms especially when he suggested we leave the lake area. Wanted us to go someplace more private. But I was thrilled he wanted to be with me, a high school girl. I told him about this cave. I've come here before. Flex, he's Aiden's best friend. His grandparents own this place . . ."

"I know."

"I had been here with Aiden to, well . . . you know. So, Chad and I walked up the river to here. I guess I kinda hoped Flex's girlfriend would see us splitting off from the group at the lake and tell Aiden. I figured once she saw I had left she'd phone him or something. Then Aiden would find me, get jealous, and we'd make up. Dumb, right?"

Wanda nodded, ignoring the pain at the back of her skull. "I'm not here to judge you, Sandie."

Her eyes shimmered with fresh tears. "Really?" She wiped her nose on her sleeve. "Anyway, he didn't show, and I got angry. So, I stayed with Chad. One thing led to another and, well, we spent the night in the cave. The next morning, Flex and Aiden found us. They jumped

Chad and start laying into him. Chad broke loose as I screamed. They chased him upstream over that tiny waterfall and started in on him again. I threw pebbles, yelling for them to stop it. I even threw one of my shoes. It hit Aiden in the chest. He tossed it down then started for me. Flex yanked him away, told him I wasn't worth the effort." Her lips quivered as she stared at her knees. "They left Chad slumped over in the brook and ran off. He had a split lip and blood ran down his chin . . ." She stopped and gulped in a sob.

"So, you tried to stop the bleeding with your sock."

Sandie blinked. "Yeah. How did you . . . Oh. Yeah. You found it."

"And my friends found your other one."

She nodded. "I filled that one with the cool water from the creek and put it to his eye. It had started to swell. We made it downstream toward the cave, then he stopped and shoved me away. Told me he didn't need this drama, called me some horrid names, and headed off. He slung the sock onto a branch as he waded off upstream. I don't know why. His car at the lake was in the other direction."

"But you let him figure that one out, right?" Wanda winked at her.

She smirked. "Yeah, I was pretty hurt and mad."

"Sandie, did he still have the other sock to his lip when he stomped off upstream?"

She thought for a moment. "Yes, I believe he did."

"Then I bet he jammed it into the shoe Aiden threw down. The one we found wedged into the riverbed just above the little waterfall."

Sandie shrugged. "I didn't try to find it. I honestly didn't like those shoes. I bought them for the hike, and they hurt my feet. I prefer to go barefoot in the summertime anyway."

That explained why she never retrieved it or her socks. Wanda squeezed the girl's hand. "Why didn't you go home?"

"Too far to walk. Besides, my mom would only cry while my dad yelled at me. They're very religious and think, well . . . let's just say I'd be an embarrassment to them." She picked at a thread on her jeans where her knees poked through. "I needed time to think. There is no cell phone reception down here. I walked downstream until I got some bars. But my battery ran really low, so instead I texted Ginger. She's my best friend. She told me the cops were looking for me. I got scared and made her swear not to tell. Then I came back here."

"You've been here alone since Friday? What have you done for food?"

Sandie shrugged. "I heard you ladies and remembered Martha had organized a women's retreat. So, since I knew where they hid the spare key, I snuck over to the retreat cabin that night and raided the fridge. I know it's stealing, but . . ." She sighed. "I kept thinking I should head back home. But I didn't want to get my friend in trouble for not telling anyone where I was. Besides, the thought of facing my parents. Everyone staring at me in town. Bothering the police. Causing such a scandal . . ." She raised her eyes to the stalactites above them. "I just got so scared."

Wanda sat quietly and let the girl compose herself.

She wiped her eyes and let out a long puff of breath. "I thought maybe I could sell my watch and my rings and this necklace Aiden gave me, catch a bus, and head to New Orleans. Or Jackson. Find a job. I don't know."

She returned her gaze to Wanda. The tears began to tumble in earnest. "I have made such a mess of my life. I can't go home. My parents will never forgive me." She buried her head in her knees and sobbed.

Wanda reached her good arm over and drew Sandie to her. "They love you. They may be angry, but they will forgive you."

Her sobs slowed. "You think so?"

Wanda raised her face to meet her own. "I have a daughter who has messed up big time again and again. Drugs, the wrong guys. I get angry with her, but I still love her and would do anything to help her if she came back."

Sandie wiped her eyes and shuddered. "You think

they will, too?"

"Absolutely." Wanda sighed. "Sandie. I am really hurting. My ankle is swelling and throbbing, my shoulder is burning, and my head is killing me. I need medical help."

The girl's eyes widened as if she realized for the first time how selfish she had been. "Of course, you do. I am so, so sorry." She pulled away. "I'll go get help. I promise. I won't run off and leave you here alone."

Wanda cupped her hand to the girl's cheek. "Thanks, hon. See, you're a good girl after all. You are rescuing a little old lady who needed assistance. No one is going to be mad at you for doing this for me. And here. Take my phone. It is almost fully charged."

She shoved it in the back pocket of her jeans. "Wait here. I'll be back soon with help."

"Thank you, Sandie."

Sandie smiled and ducked out of the cave.

Wanda leaned back against the rock walls and sighed. "Thank You, Lord."

Julie B Cosgrove

CHAPTER 36

An hour later, Wanda reclined on a gurney in the minor emergency clinic. Her shoulder had been slinged. Her ankle had been fitted with a soft cast. The pain meds had reduced her headache from a banging snare drum to a slight dull ache. And Todd stood by her side, his arms folded while Betty Sue fluffed her pillow and Evelyn poured her some water from a styrofoam pitcher.

"You're angry with me."

Todd huffed a long breath. "Of course, I am. If you weren't injured, I'd turn you over my knee."

Evelyn laughed. "Role reversal. How many times she wanted to do that to you in high school when you and your sister bunked in with Wanda while your parents ironed out their nasty divorce."

Wanda winked. "But you love me, anyway."

"I do, Aunt Wanda."

"I told Sandie her parents would react the same way. I hope they have."

"How did you know she was there?"

"I didn't. But something told me if I found the cave, I'd find answers. She actually found me. I must have cried out when I fell."

She thanked Evelyn for the cup of water and took a sip. What a difference a few hours made. Not too long ago she had prayed for the water to go away. Now she craved it to cool her parched throat.

"I am glad you came to Louisiana, Todd."

"Me, too. But you are riding home with me. No arguments. Betty Sue and Evelyn will tandem with us in your car."

"Deal." No way did she want to attempt to drive with these injuries. "As long as we stop off at that mega convenience store in Longview for fudge."

Evelyn hooted. "Now I know she's better."

Betty Sue smiled for the first time. "Sure you don't want to get an apple?"

"Um, Yes. I think it will be a while before pink lady apples are appealing to me again."

"A-peeling?" Evelyn groaned at the pun.

Wanda pushed the button to raise the head of her gurney a bit more. "So, Todd, where did you dash off to?"

"Chad walked into the police department and

confessed everything."

"Teenage drama. But why did Humphrey want you?"

"Humphrey figured I might be less of a threat when he interviewed Chad, seeing I am younger and not from this area. I was more than willing to help. He told us about the cave and how he was beaten up. Assured us he left Sandie unharmed. And insisted he would not be pressing charges against Flex and Aiden. They were only trying to protect Sandie and he might have done the same given the situation. Plus, he instigated it by calling them and Sandie some pretty foul names."

"Bet it relieved Officer Mulligan. He didn't have to order his son's arrest." Wanda scoffed. "And Humphrey is probably glad to get everyone from her parents to the governor off his neck, too."

"I hope Chad learned his lesson about picking up high school girls." Betty Sue clucked her tongue.

Wanda agreed. She turned back to Todd. "There is one thing I don't understand, though."

He hiked his hip onto the edge of the gurney. "Yeah?"

"Olga."

"Ah." He grinned. "Turns out we were wrong. No one hit her, Aunt Wanda."

Wanda blinked. Had she heard him correctly?

Evelyn's mouth swung open, and Betty Sue inched

closer.

"Seems when she leaned over to open the glove box to get her cell phone USB cord, her phone slipped to the baseboard. She reached for it, loss her balance, and whacked her own head on the console." He snickered. "Took a while for the dust to clear, I guess. When she climbed into Rachel McDavid's car to head back to the retreat, she stared at Rachel's glove box. That's when it dawned on her what really happened."

"Which is why she wanted to speak to Humphrey in private."

Evelyn snapped her fingers. "And why she acted so weird. Embarrassment over causing such a fuss."

Todd bobbed his head. "By the way, Martha and Rachel did confess they were eavesdropping. But only to see if you three had actually figured out where Sandie had gone off to. Neither had any miscreant motives."

"Oh?" Wanda still had her doubts.

"They figured out Flex had given ya'll the clues so he must have known her whereabouts. But they were afraid of getting Flex and Aiden in trouble since both had received wrestling scholarships for college. Martha is Aiden's aunt, by the way. Her sister is married to Officer Mulligan."

Betty Sue sighed. "Guess we need to give them both a bit of grace, then. Tough position to be in."

"I imagine." Wanda rolled her eyes. "So, Mulligan

gave the socks and shoe back to George to find out if it contained Sandie's blood or someone else's, right? You guess Mulligan knew his son, Aiden had beat up Chad?"

"Speculation. He isn't saying. Simply said he forgot to let Humphrey know about the socks and shoe. He became busy with another case and then several fender-benders during the storm and got behind in his paperwork."

Wanda let it drop. Not her concern, really, how the cops interacted in West Monroe. "And the crossword puzzles?"

"Flex admitted he gave y'all a new one, hoping it would lead you to the painting in the Room Five where you'd be staying and then discover the note and find the cave. If ya'll had, then you would have found Sandie and hopefully Chad. Since you were strangers, and pardon me, 'little old ladies', you might not spook them as much. His words."

The three glanced at each other and simultaneously rolled their eyes.

Todd coughed into his fist then continued. "Flex worried that Chad might have been more injured than he turned out to be, but again he was afraid to come forward and lose his scholarship chances. Or snitch on his best friend."

"I still want to speak with Flex about his talent for designing word puzzles."

Todd patted her arm. "Rachel gave me his cell phone number. I think he's still interested in the gig, too."

The ER doctor came in and stood at the foot of the gurney. "Well, good news, Mrs. Warner. No concussion. You wrenched your shoulder and ankle. No breaks, though. No torn ligaments. Just sprained muscles. I want you to take it easy for a week or so, okay? And follow up with your own doctor within the next two days." He glanced at her then typed into his laptop.

"So, when can I get out of here?" Wanda lifted her chin.

The doctor winked. "I'm writing up your discharge instructions now. Whenever you say the word."

She threw back the sheet. "Let's go."

Evelyn peered at her. "That's two words."

Wanda laughed harder than she had in a long while.

Acknowledgments

I am so thankful for Write Integrity Press agreeing to continue the Wordplay Mysteries series. Writing about Wanda and her friends is a joy. I hope you enjoyed their adventure on the retreat as they went "away with words."

Thanks to Shirley Crowder who edited this one, and to Marji Laine who is such an amazing graphic cover artist as well as publisher.

I would like to thank my son, James, who helped me brainstorm the ending while we were stranded in my apartment during a North Texas ice storm. Since I was recovering from minor surgery, he also waited on me hand and foot. And to Katy Huth Jones, my Scrabble partner, who also let me bounce ideas off of her. If you also happen to like epic Medieval novels with damsels, knights, and dragons, check out her Mercy series.

I also want to thank the ladies of Good Shepherd Anglican in West Monroe. Several years ago, I was invited to lead their retreat at a family cabin in Northern Louisiana and that experience gave me the basis for some of the fictitious surroundings for this novel.

I would be negligent if I didn't thank God for blessing me with the means to do what I love, writing fun clean mystery novels that honor Him.

Last, but hardly least, I thank you, dear reader, for

purchasing and reading this book. I hope you will read the others in this series, if you have not already, and I would greatly appreciate any honest review online at Amazon or Goodreads as well as sharing your thoughts with your friends on social media.

May you always know that love opens the doors for forgiveness, and show others the grace none of us deserve but so desperately need.

Now may our Lord Jesus Christ himself, and God our Father, who loved us and gave us eternal comfort and good hope through grace, comfort your hearts and establish them in every good work and word (2 Thessalonians 2: 16-17).

About the Author

Whodunnit? My mom used to ask us that with a hand cocked on her hip, peering into our wide-eyed faces. Naturally the blame trickled down to the youngest one—me. I had to solve the crime so I could plead my innocence.

On walks through the Texas Hill Country with my dad, I became a keen observer of nature, and later in life as an adult and writer, of human nature. So sleuthing is part of my DNA.

I wrote award-winning works in high school creative writing class, but then life edged in. Even so, on my long commutes I'd make up storylines in my head. After my husband passed away, the desire to write returned. My sister suggested I write mysteries, which had long been my favorite genre.

Now I absorb mysteries whenever I get the chance then let the whodunnits capture my imagination, and my keyboard. I think I'm finally becoming who God intended me to be.

Besides writing mystery, suspense-romance, and

short stories, I am an editor for two Christian publishing companies as well as a freelance editor. For the past twelve years, I have regularly written for several devotional publications. My own blog, *Where Did You Find God Today*, has readers in over 50 countries. Visit my website at www.juliebcosgrove.com

Other Wordplay Mysteries:

Word Has It – Not prone to gossip, Wanda keeps herself to herself. But when she hears from her nephew that a ring of thieves may be hiding out in the area, she begins to wonder if the old Ferguson place is still abandoned. When words like jewels, woodshed, landing, and evil appear on their weekly word game days after a deadly shooting on the property, she determines it is a sign she and her friends should investigate.

Word Gets Around – Each of the three ladies receive a nonsensical note slipped between the wiper blades of their cars. When the ladies combine the words on a word game board, it spells trouble for one of Betty's former students, who is now a freelance reporter for the *Oakmont County Gazette*. Could it be she reported way too much?

In Other Words – Many English words contain the same letters but in different order, like stressed and desserts. After the local store owner is found dead in the alley, the ladies will need their word playing skills to unravel the dual meanings of the graffiti that appears around town before two more people's games end.

Hang On Every Word – Wanda lands a gig as the word puzzle designer for the local newspaper. Then the answers to her clues end up relating to crimes in the downtown stores. Some merchants wonder if she is feeding the crooks the answers so she can get credit for solving more mysteries. Will Todd be pressured into arresting his own aunt?

And be sure to watch for Book Six, *Loss for Words*. Betty Sue and Wanda find a disheveled woman walking along the highway. She has no memory of how she got there. But she does have a nasty goose egg on her head and a ripped up cryptic classified ad in her pocket. How could the SOWS (Scrub Oak Widows Society) not help this amnesiac find out what happened?

During a garage sale to help fund the poor lady's medical bills, Wanda finds more cryptic newsprint words taped to the bottom of several donated objects. If they piece together what happened, will one of them end up wandering on the highway, too… or suffer an even worse fate?

Mystery and Suspense
by Write Integrity Press

Thank you
for reading our books!

Please consider leaving a review for the author
on the purchase page for this book.

Look for other books
published by

P

Pursued Books
an imprint of

W

Write Integrity Press
www.WriteIntegrity.com